SO-AFJ-792

Vashti was alone. Her peaceful childhood in the farming village was gone forever. As she wandered the swarming *bustee* (slum) of Calcutta, India, each day was a scramble to find enough food to stay alive.

Then Miss Narain, a Christian, brought something the Hindu goddess Lakshmi had never brought—a new start, an escape from the fear and sadness that overwhelmed her.

Here is the vivid story of life, love and faith in a land unknown to most Americans and Canadians. You'll remember VASHTI AND THE STRANGE GOD long after this book returns to your shelf.

Vashti
and the strange God

Gladys Moon Cook

David C. Cook Publishing Co.
ELGIN, ILLINOIS—WESTON, ONTARIO

Vashti and the Strange God
Copyright © 1975 David C. Cook Publishing Co.
First Printing, August 1975
Second Printing, March 1976

All rights reserved. Except for brief excerpts for
review purposes, no part of this book may be reproduced
or used in any form or by any means—electronic or
mechanical, including photocopying, recording, or
information storage and retrieval systems—without
written permission from the publisher.

David C. Cook Publishing Co., Elgin, IL 60120

Printed in the United States of America
Library of Congress Catalog Number: 74-29465

ISBN: 0-912692-57-X

To my Son, Bruce,
who persuaded me
to take up writing

CONTENTS

1

A New Life Begins

Vashti Prakash, lying on her cot in the darkened hostel room, clamped her hand over her mouth to keep the sobs inside. It was her first night at the boarding school—a Christian boarding school. She felt utterly alone yet she would not, she simply would not, let these girls whose cots lined the wall know how homesick she was. Thirteen years old and never having been to school before, she faced plenty of problems without being labeled a mama's baby.

Yet it was for her mother and little sister, Meenu, she yearned as she lay in the darkness of this strange room. Mama, back in Calcutta, would be stretched out on her frayed quilts sleeping the sleep of the exhausted. Perhaps the gnawing of a rat would rouse her and she would draw Meenu close to protect her from the rodent's bite.

When her mother had told her good-bye before she left to go to work, she had begun coughing. Vashti knew the separation had upset her and brought on the attack. She hoped it hadn't been so bad that she had started bleeding. The mistress who hired Mama as a sweeper (a maid in a home), was very annoyed when her help bled. It slowed down their work.

How Vashti wished she had even a small likeness of the goddess Lakshmi so she could worship her. At home, she had always tried to take over as much work as possible to make it easier for Mama. Now she couldn't even pray for her! When they had lived in the village there had been a shrine of the family's goddess only three miles from their home and Vashti worshiped there often.

How would she ever be able to pray in this strange place? She dared not walk out in search of a shrine or temple. When she was not attending classes or studying she must work in payment for her meals. Miss Narain, who was employed by the Christian Brotherhood of Sharing had arranged for her tuition and hostel room, knowing she was of the Hindu religion. In her eagerness for an education Vashti hadn't thought how hard it might be for one of another faith to attend a Christian school. Would she be permitted to worship as a Hindu girl?

Vashti heard a kind of scampering noise and she cried out unthinkingly. The girl who lay on the cot nearest her reached out and touched her gently.

"Do not be afraid. It is just the branches of the

tamarind tree scraping the roof," she said.

"Forgive me for waking you," Vashti said in a low voice. "I thought the noise was a rat and I'm afraid of their bite."

The friendly girl let her hand lay where it was on Vashti's arm. "There are no rats in the hostel or school," she whispered. "Miss Adhikari has cats that keep the rats away. Is this your first time away from home?"

"Yes," Vashti murmured.

"I am Radha Gopal."

"I am Vashti Prakash," Vashti answered.

"Have you gone to school?" Radha asked.

"No, but I can read and write."

"You will like it here. The teachers are kind."

Radha moved her hand and placed it under her cheek. Soon Vashti heard the even rhythm of her breathing and she knew her new friend was asleep.

Vashti lay awake for quite some time after that, but the terrible feeling of aloneness was gone. She had said she could read and write. Now her mind conjured up words, numbers and small addition, subtraction and division problems in arithmetic. These thoughts led her back to the days when her father had land and grew millet and tended his own rice paddy. That was when they lived in the village, Bajribasha. For more than a year now, when she wanted to escape the horrors of the things she had seen since they were forced to leave their farm, she brought her mind to dwell upon life in the village.

There was a government school on the outskirts of Savonkota, the town just six miles from Bajribasha. The principal had come to talk to *Baba* (father) about

11

entering Govind, Vashti's brother, in classes there. Vashti wanted to hear about the school but it would not be proper for her to show herself while the men talked. She had hidden herself behind the curtained door and listened. The principal, who had to be a man of learning, seemed almost a god to the girl. *Baba* had never held with education but the man explained that Govind could make a much better marriage if he had schooling. Her father would give heed to this argument, Vashti knew. How she yearned for knowledge herself but, of course, the school was for boys only.

"You are sure an education will bring a bride with a bigger dowry?" *Baba* asked the principal.

"I have known cases with people of your caste where it brought even 700 more rupees," the teacher said.

"He will be at school next Monday," her father said.

After the principal had left, *Baba* called loudly, "Gauri!"

Vashti's mother dropped her hoe where she worked in the garden and hurried into the house. "Yes, husband," she said.

"The boy goes to school on Monday. See that he is ready," Mr. Prakash said.

"To school?" Vashti's mother looked at Govind. "But he is so small and the school is far away."

"He is almost six. He is not too young to walk a few miles," *Baba* said.

Mrs. Prakash would cross her husband's wishes if she felt she must but it was not her nature to do so. Now she spoke timidly. "I fear he will lose his way."

Vashti spoke confidently. "I will take my brother to school."

12

Baba paid no attention to her. "Don't talk foolishly," he said to his wife. "Govind needs only to follow the road. It will lead him to the school."

In her eagerness, Vashti went to her father and took hold of his sleeve. "I know the way there. It is three miles beyond the shrine. I will walk with Govind to school every day."

Baba looked at her. "You are getting to be a big girl. It shall be as you say. You will walk with him the first few times."

"But how will Govind come home?" Mama asked.

"I'll wait outside till school is out. Then I will walk home with him."

Now Vashti had grown so drowsy that her thoughts and dreams intermingled as she lay on her cot that first night away from home. "It is this strange thing I lie upon," she thought. "It causes me to be asleep and yet awake. I would much rather have a mat and sleep on the floor."

Finally dreams took over entirely and she walked with Govind to the mud-walled schoolhouse. Then she saw a small girl who was herself standing outside the window straining to hear a few words from the recitation of the class within.

Going to sleep so late, Vashti did not waken until Radha spoke her name.

"Oh, I let the sun beat me up. And Miss Adhikari may have had work for me to do," she said, embarrassed before her new friend.

The girls looked at one another with curiosity as well as interest. They had talked in darkness the night before and this was the first time they had actually seen one another.

13

Radha saw that the new girl was about her height but reedlike in build. She admired the bigness of Vashti's dark brown eyes but thought it a pity that they seemed to be sunk within a cavity, so tightly was the skin drawn over the framework of her facial bones. Her features were regular and her hair was jet black.

Vashti thought Radha appeared to be a happy girl. There was something a little foreign-looking about her. Her skin was far lighter than Vashti's. Her eyes were brown-gold and her mouth was generous in size. It looked like a mouth that could shape itself into a smile very easily.

"Miss Adhikari won't expect you to work before breakfast. None of us do," she told Vashti.

"Are you a part-time worker, too?"

"Yes. I couldn't stay here if I didn't work for my board. My family is very poor," Radha told her.

"Mine, too," Vashti said. She felt she was giving a false impression. She wasn't telling Radha how desperately poor the Prakashes were. She felt sure her new friend had never known a girl before who had begged on the streets of Calcutta. But she couldn't lay herself open to the contempt of the students here at school. She would never tell her real circumstances.

Now she put her skirt to rights and the two girls left the hostel.

"We brush our teeth in the courtyard," Radha told her. "Have you a twig of *neem?*"

"Yes, thank you." For Miss Narain from the Brotherhood of Sharing had supplied her with twigs as well as an eating bowl and all the clothing she had brought to the school. "Are you of the Hindu religion?" she asked Radha.

"I am a Christian," Radha answered. "My father is a Christian minister."

Vashti felt badly to learn that this kind girl was not of her faith. Vashti's father would never approve of her being on good terms with a Christian.

She turned to search the faces of other girls as they polished their teeth. None wore the Hindu symbol on her forehead. This did not mean that none were of her faith. She was of the Vaisya caste and the Sudras were lower in caste than she. Only the Brahmans and the Kshatriyas, the two highest castes, wore the round dot called *tiki* that identified them as being of the Hindu religion.

Her searching look brought her a surprise because she saw a child no more than six years old standing near the cook's shed.

"Is that little girl a student here?" she asked Radha.

"Yes. The older one beside her is her sister. They are orphans. Their uncle sent them here. He had no wife so he could not keep them with him," Radha told her.

"Are there many here who are so young?" Vashti asked.

"She is the only one who boards but a great number come from town," Radha said.

How wonderful it would be if Meenu, her own baby sister, could be with her, Vashti thought. Meenu was not really a baby except in mind because she was eight years old. *Baba* called her a natural fool and her presence was intolerable to him. Luckily, Mama's mistress permitted her to bring Meenu with her when she came to work. Little sister was content to sit and play with a rag or string or anything handed to her. She was never any bother.

15

Now, Radha led Vashti to the water tap where they washed and then they joined the line of girls waiting with their bowls for breakfast. The cook ladled a dipper of thick rice water into each bowl and handed each girl a slice of bread. Vashti's eyes grew wide at so much food for breakfast. During the last year she had no more than this for a whole day's sustenance. She would grow fat if she ate this much three times a day.

As she sopped up the last bit of rice water with her bread, an older girl came to her.

"Are you Vashti Prakash?" she asked.

"Yes," Vashti said.

"Miss Adhikari wants to talk to you. I'll take you there," the girl said.

Vashti had seen Miss Adhikari, the principal, only briefly the night before. Miss Narain had brought her here and it was very late when they arrived. No one was about but the principal who had been waiting for them in her office. She led Vashti across the courtyard to the hostel.

"We won't turn on the lights for the girls will be sleeping," she had said.

She lit a candle and they had gone up a flight of stairs. The flickering light showed they were in a long room where girls lay on cots lined along the wall. Miss Adhikari took Vashti to a corner where there was an empty bed made up. "This will be your space from now on," she had said. Then she hung the girl's extra clothing on hooks set into the wall opposite.

"Will you be all right now?" she had asked in a low voice.

"Yes," Vashti had answered, her eyes downcast as was proper for one in a lower station of life. She

16

regarded Miss Adhikari with near reverence. Was she not so well educated that she was at the head of a large school?

"Then I will leave you. Sleep well."

As Miss Adhikari started to leave, Vashti bowed to the floor in obeisance.

The principal stopped her. "Please, no. We do not do such things here in this school. We are all sisters as God intended us to be." With that, she hurried away.

All sisters? How could she say that? Miss Adhikari must surely be of the Brahman caste and Vashti was only a Vaisya. She thought she would never be able to understand such strange people as Christians.

When she lay down on the strange cot she felt desolated. All her life she had known her position in regard to other people. Suddenly this assurance as well as her family were taken from her. She might have wished to return home and submit to the despair of life in Calcutta had not Radha shown friendliness at the right moment.

Now the bright sun of morning changed her attitude. She approached the principal's office worried only that she might be put in the class with the six-year-olds. As she had told Radha, she had never been to school but she had shared her brother's books when he had been a student.

Raising her folded hands to her breast, she greeted Miss Adhikari with a *namaste*—an Indian greeting meaning "peace." It was not an obeisance and she hoped the principal would not object. She was pleased when Miss Adhikari returned the greeting.

Miss Adhikari sat at her desk that was covered with weighted stacks of papers. Vashti could see there must be a great deal of work involved in running a school and a hostel, too.

"Please sit down." The principal motioned Vashti to a chair.

Vashti sat down in it but she felt awkward. When they had lived in the village, *Baba* had owned a chair but he seldom sat in it. It was a canvas chair that had once belonged to *Tata* (grandfather). The chair was very old and the family feared the cloth would split so *Baba* sat on the smooth-packed floor like the rest.

"We must decide what grade to put you in," Miss Adhikari said. "Miss Narain said you had learned to read from your brother's books."

"Yes, I read all of his books. At first he had to explain what the teacher had told them about the letters in the words, but soon I was able to read without help," Vashti explained.

"How far did your brother go in school?"

"He was in fourth grade. He could not go to school after we left the village," Vashti told her.

"I see. Well, I have prepared some exercises for you and we will see how you get along."

Miss Adhikari brought her a sheaf of papers and a board to write upon. "Take your time in answering. I will leave you but I'll come back later." She started to go out of the room and then she turned. "If you would be more comfortable sitting on the floor, please do."

"Thank you," Vashti said, and moved to sit cross-legged on the matting.

Vashti had written in all the answers and made a few corrections when Miss Adhikari returned and took the papers. Vashti was not nervous because the answers had seemed very simple.

19

Miss Adhikari went through them quickly. "I will place you in the fifth grade," she said. "I don't think you will find it beyond you. Now, let us talk about your duties. Since you once lived on a farm perhaps you would like to work in the garden."

Nothing could have pleased Vashti more. It would seem like home to plant the seeds in the dark, crumbling soil and, later, watch the delicate green shoots come through the earth. She had done this back in Bajribasha. She hoped there would be plenty of water so that she could moisten the ground every night when the plants were young and needed all the help they could get. "I would like garden work," she said.

"Good. But the garden will not keep you busy all the time. Perhaps you can help with the milking."

"Once we owned a goat when we lived in Bajribasha and I learned to milk it," Vashti said.

"We have buffaloes, three of them. Their milk is used in cooking as well as drinking and they supply the *ghee* (butter) for our table," Miss Adhikari explained.

At mention of three buffaloes, Vashti blanched. She had never been around buffaloes and they seemed such huge animals. Would she dare to sit near enough to one to milk it? "I have never milked an *arna* (Indian species of buffalo). I'll try," she said bravely.

"Go out with Mrs. Ghose and the other girls a few times and acquaint yourself with the animals. You must lose your uneasiness about them before you put your hand to their teats," Miss Adhikari said. "And now it is time for our noontime dinner. Don't forget your bowl."

2

The Strange and Only God

After lunch, when Miss Adhikari walked with Vashti to the garden plot, she said, "Mrs. Ghose is a Dravidian."

Vashti had no idea what a Dravidian was but she wanted to show politeness to the principal. She could think of nothing better to say than, "Yes."

When she came face to face with Mrs. Ghose, she stared fascinated. The woman was one of those rare specimens in India, a fat woman. Not only fat but huge in every way. She was almost a head taller then Miss Adhikari. Her hands and feet and shoulders were man-size. But it was not the height or breadth of the lady that made Vashti gape. It was her blue-black color.

Her skin shone like black ivory. She wore no head covering and her thick glossy hair was braided and bound at the nape of her neck. Vashti had seen dark Indians in Calcutta but never one so black.

"Mrs. Ghose, I've brought you a worker," Miss Adhikari said.

Mrs. Ghose laid down her hoe and came to greet them.

"This is Vashti Prakash," Miss Adhikari said. "She is a new student in our school."

Every part that made up Mrs. Ghose's face broke into a smile. "You want to work where you can help seeds grow into food?" she asked.

Overwhelmed, Vashti could only murmur, "Yes."

"She will come to you tomorrow at three," Miss Adhikari told her. She walked along the garden's edge. "The cabbages are doing well," she said, "and so are the pumpkins."

"And there will be plenty of chili peppers to tickle your girls' palates," Mrs. Ghose said.

Vashti marveled that two women could be so different. Miss Adhikari's size contrasted to Mrs. Ghose's bulk. The principal was no more than five feet tall and delicately boned. The girl had felt certain the head of the school was a Brahman, not only because she was a teacher and light-skinned but because her facial features were like those of the aristocratic ladies who rode through Calcutta streets in automobiles. Miss Adhikari seemed very serious but Mrs. Ghose's sharply chisled features were laced with laugh wrinkles.

"I don't get out to the garden as often as I'd like to," Miss Adhikari said. "And now I must hurry off. I'll

22

send Vashti to you at milking time. She will get acquainted with our buffaloes and perhaps she will be a milker later."

The principal took the new girl to the different teachers of her classes and she was assigned lessons for the next day. Vashti learned that Hindi was the language of the lower grades. From eighth through the tenth grades the girls studied from English texts and only English was spoken in the classrooms. Vashti would study English, mathematics, grammar, spelling and geography. In fifth grade, geography concerned only India.

"Have you ever studied geography?" Miss Adhikari asked.

"No," Vashti admitted.

"It is sad but most people of India know very little about their own country. This course will tell about the people and their customs as well as the land."

"Do you teach the class?" Vashti asked.

"No. I teach only in the upper grades. Except for religion. I have a class in Christianity and I am in charge of chapel. We have 300 students enrolled in school and all are required to attend weekday chapel. I don't want you to think of this as a duty. It is a privilege. And of course you know we don't insist that our girls become Christian."

Vashti thought this was the time to ask if she might go to a shrine to worship in her own way. Somehow, she couldn't ask it. Small as Miss Adhikari was, she was more overwhelming than Mrs. Ghose. She walked alongside the principal and nothing was said until they arrived at the office. Miss Adhikari handed her the books she would need, a tablet and two pencils.

"Today you have until suppertime to spend on your lessons. You may study in the courtyard or on the veranda. If you like, you may go back to the hostel."

"Thank you," Vashti said. Carrying her treasured books, she started toward the building where she had slept the night before.

Sitting cross-legged on the floor at the foot of her cot, she spread her books about her. She was eager to begin, yet she had trouble deciding which one she should start with. Geography, that was the one. Perhaps it would tell her what a Dravidian was. Even after seeing Mrs. Ghose, she wasn't sure. Was she called a Dravidian because she was big or was it because she was black? Or maybe it was neither of these. Perhaps a Dravidian was a person with sorcery powers. Surely there was room in her body to hold her own spirit and another one, too. Had she been entrusted with the *atman* (essence or spirit) of a goddess or god? Vashti's mother had once known a person who had the power of the evil goddess, Kali. If Mrs. Ghose was a sorceress, Vashti hoped her gift was not for evil.

But this was nonsense. She had no reason to think the black woman was a witch. Her eyes, her whole face, showed nothing but good humor and kindness. She opened her book and studied the lesson for the next day but it told her nothing about a Dravidian. She went on to prepare for her other classes.

Vashti, with the help of her brother's books, had taught herself to read and write very well. Now she absorbed knowledge from her textbooks as the soil soaks up rain after a long drought. She was just finishing her last arithmetic problem when Radha

24

Gopal came in. Radha laid her books down and unrolled a picture she carried.

"Look what my father sent me today," she said.

Vashti looked and saw the picture of a man with flowing hair and beard. He was a handsome man but she was most aware of his eyes. They were gentle and full of understanding.

"Is he a priest?" she asked.

"He is Jesus," Radha said. "I forgot you are not Christian so you would not know about Him. He is God's Son and God sent Him to teach us the way to live so that we can be with Him in Heaven."

"Which God?" Vashti asked.

"We Christians know that there is but one God and He is Father and Creator of all things," Radha answered. She tacked the picture above her cot.

"Now you have a shrine and you can pray to your Christian God," Vashti said enviously.

"A shrine is not necessary. I can pray no matter where I am or what I am doing," Radha told her. "But I love Jesus and His picture reminds me to do what is right."

If the Christian God was not angered when a girl divided her time between the thing she was doing and the prayer she offered, he was a very strange god, Vashti thought. She opened her English book and studied the way that English letters were formed.

"Oh, I forgot to tell you, Miss Adhikari sent word that it is time for milking. Are you going to be a milker?" Radha said.

"I'm not sure, but I'm going with Mrs. Ghose and watch her milk this evening," Vashti answered.

"I'd be afraid to be near those big buffaloes, but

Lata and Shoba, two girls in our hostel room, are milkers," Radha said. "I'd better take you there myself. Mrs. Ghose will already be at the shed."

The two girls left the hostel and started down the path that led past the garden on the way to the milk shed.

"One of the girls claimed she saw a cobra in the grass near here. She probably didn't. It was Purnima and she doesn't always tell the truth. But since then I've been careful when I walk near here," Radha said.

Vashti shivered. She was afraid of snakes and especially the cobra because it was a sacred snake and couldn't be killed. Her father said it was useful; it killed rats and mice and bugs that were harmful to the crops. He had told his family how to protect themselves from its fangs and now she passed the information on to Radha.

"A cobra strikes forward and it can't strike any other way. You will be safer if you jump quickly to its side," she said.

"That's a good thing to know," Radha answered. "And here we are at the milk shed. I'll go back and study now."

Vashti approached Mrs. Ghose where she sat on her stool and kept a stream of milk flowing from the buffalo's udder to the milk vessel.

"I'm sorry I'm late," Vashti said.

"You are here only to watch and there is plenty of time for that," Mrs. Ghose answered.

The other girls were seated close to their animals and the buffaloes themselves were placidly chewing hay.

"They look big," Vashti said.

"No, no. These *arna* are a small breed. And gentle."

27

"Aren't you afraid to sit so near? What if a bee should sting its leg and it gave a kick?" Vashti asked.

"What if an automobile on the streets of Calcutta should run over you when you go home on holiday?" Mrs. Ghose answered.

"I see what you mean. There is always danger of some kind. And this *arna* doesn't look fierce when you see it close."

"It is no more fierce than a cow. Its head is like a cow's, don't you think?" Mrs. Ghose patted her animal affectionately. "They love us. All three of them do. They know we are their friends because we feed them well." She stopped now and looked at Vashti critically. "You could use a little feeding yourself. Put your head down here and open your mouth."

Vashti did as she was told and Mrs. Ghose sent a gusher of milk into the opening. Vashti sputtered and wiped her face with the hem of her skirt. "It's warm," she said.

"Warm and good," Mrs. Ghose answered. "More of that will put flesh on your bones. And now you and my two girl helpers go wash for dinner," Mrs. Ghose said.

"Are they through milking?" Vashti asked.

"They should be," she said. "Lata! Shoba! Bring your milk if you are finished."

The girls came with their vessels of milk balanced gracefully on their heads.

"This is the new student, Vashti Prakash," Mrs. Ghose said.

"Hello, Vashti, I'm Lata. We live in the same room at the hostel," one of them said.

"And I'm Shoba," the other added. Her face was deeply pocked with smallpox scars.

28

Vashti folded her hands in the *namaste* greeting and the three started down the path toward the house.

"Isn't Mrs. Ghose coming?" Vashti asked.

"No. She goes home for supper. She lives in Lorabad," Shoba said.

"But she won't go home until she has given each one of the *arnas* a good rubbing," Lata added.

"Does she have far to walk?" Vashti asked.

"Not far. Our day students come from there," Lata said. "They don't eat supper with us either."

When Vashti joined the line with her bowl she stood between Lata and Shoba. Cook filled their bowls with chopped vegetables and milk curds and handed a *loochi* (fried wheatcake) to each one.

"Miss Adhikari must be rich to feed us so well," Vashti remarked.

"The money isn't hers. Most of it comes from the Christian Brotherhood of Sharing. And they get it from Christians all over the world," Lata explained.

"Some people like to know who they are helping and they send money to Miss Adhikari instead of the Christian Brotherhood. I have a sponsor in America," Shoba said.

"It is good of Christians to give girls a chance to learn," Vashti said.

When supper was over, all the girls went to the rooms where they slept. "We study until ten o'clock and then the lights go off," Radha told Vashti.

Vashti had completed her assignments in the afternoon but she opened her arithmetic book and began working problems beyond the lesson. She paused in her work to look at Radha's picture of Jesus. The light upon His face changed His expression to one of sadness but the kindness was still there.

As she bent over her problems again, a girl came to stand near her.

"Vashti, this is Purnima," Radha said.

Again, Vashti folded her hands in the *namaste.* "That is an old-fashioned way to meet people," Purnima said.

"I'm sorry if I offended you," Vashti said.

"You don't offend me. You don't concern me that much," Purnima retorted. "Let me see what you are doing in mats."

"Mats?" Vashti looked puzzled.

"Mathematics, goose. Don't you know anything?" Vashti handed her the book.

Purnima laughed. "This is baby stuff." She read the problem aloud.

"Mr. Narvankar bought six young bullocks and paid 25 *rupees* each. How much did he pay for all?"

"I am beginning in fifth grade," Vashti said, embarrassed.

"Fifth grade? You look older than I, and I am in sixth grade. See, this is my mats paper for tomorrow," Purnima said.

Vashti took the problems offered her and read the first one. Then thoughtfully, she read it again.

"Mr. Charon used one *ser* (measure) of millet seed to plant one and a half acres of land. How many *ser* will he need to plant six acres in millet?"

Purnima had given the answer as being three *ser*.

"Oh, you should change this before you give the paper to your teacher tomorrow. The answer is not right," Vashti exclaimed.

"What do you mean, it isn't right? It is three *ser* just

30

like I said. You don't know anything about sixth grade mats," Purnima declared.

"But it can't be," Vashti argued. She felt she had to make her see her mistake. "If one *ser* of millet would sow one and a half acres, the farmer would need two *ser* to sow three acres. It would take twice as many *ser* to plant six acres and that would be four *ser.*"

By now, another girl from the sixth grade had joined Vashti, Purnima and Radha.

"She is right, Purnima. I have the same answer that she got," the newcomer said.

"I knew it was four. I just made a mistake when I wrote down three," Purnima said and walked away.

"If you can work sixth grade problems, you should be in sixth grade," the girl said. "What is your name?"

"Let me introduce you two," Radha said. "Shantha, this is Vashti Prakash."

"I think the teacher will soon move you out of fifth grade, Vashti," Shantha said. "Now, I'd better start studying or I'll be back with you."

Vashti stacked her books and lay down on her cot. She was sorry now that she had told Purnima about the error on her paper. To have a fifth grader point out a mistake was naturally embarrassing to a sixth grader. But on the whole, it had been a good day.

She stole another look at the picture Radha had tacked on the wall. How she wished she had a shrine of the goddess Lakshmi so that she could pray for her family's safety and health. Her heavy eyelids told her sleep was near. "Good night Mama, good night Meenu, good night Govind." She remembered her duty and whispered good night to *Baba* before she drifted off.

31

3

Bitter Memories

"Oh, here is the little one who fears buffaloes but may yet learn to care for them." It was Mrs. Ghose's greeting to Vashti when she came to the garden the next day. "You are ready now to hoe the hard earth so that the plant roots can breathe?"

"Yes," Vashti answered.

Mrs. Ghose handed her a hoe. "Let us look at the garden," she said. "See, we have lentils, cabbages, beets, corn, sweet potatoes, pumpkins and chili peppers. You may start hoeing the corn."

Vashti went to the end of the row and started downward. The rhythmic striking of blade on hard dirt held her attention for a while. She felt the hot sun on

33

her back while sweat dripped from her face and it was good. It was like her old home where she worked beside her mother in the plot near the house while *Baba* tended the millet in the fields.

She thought of the problem in Purnima's book—Mr. Charon used one *ser* of millet seed to plant one and one half acres of land. Here was a problem that would never find its way into a book: If a man should go to the moneylender and borrow 500 *rupees*, how many years would it take for the moneylender to claim ownership to the man's farm for interest unpaid? Vashti's thoughts were bitter. *Baba* was but a small boy when a big drought came and *Tata,* unable to see his family starve, had gone to the village moneylender for aid. The loan had been a rope strangling the Prakashes ever since. Although interest was paid whenever possible, the moneylender forced the sale of the land bit by bit until the last acre and even the house in the village were gone.

Because of things that had happened to her family since then, Vashti thought she hated the moneylender. She knew she should not question any fate that befell her. Her religion taught her that good or bad fortune was of no importance. The flame of life was short and there was always the chance that the next time she existed, her life would be better. But how could she accept the change that had come to them all? Her mother had begun her coughing in the downpour of rain as they walked away from their old home. Her brother had become a beggar and she, herself, had begged. Worst of all was the change in *Baba*. He sat in the one-room hovel where they lived in the *bustee* (slums) and earned not a single *rupee* in a year's time.

When Mama came home from work he slapped her if she were slow in preparing his supper. Little Meenu, foolish though she was, had learned to find a dark corner where *Baba* would be least likely to strike her. Even Govind came in for his share of the blows, though having a son had once been the most important thing in *Baba's* life.

Yet *Baba* had not always been like this. Vashti remembered how he used to rise before dawn and eat the hastily warmed rice if there was any left over from supper. If there was none he would drink rice water or whatever Mama set before him. Then he would rouse the bullock where it slept in the courtyard and hitch it to the wooden plow. All day, except for the brief period he stopped to eat at noontime when Vashti brought him food, he would work in the field. When the sun was setting, Vashti would wait for him at the door, a towel in her hand, a pan of cool water nearby.

"Has *Baba's* little jewel been a good child today?" he would ask, touching her braids lightly with his hand.

"Yes, *Baba*," Vashti would tell him. She would flush with pleasure while Mama turned to smile at the two of them.

Then Vashti would seat herself near the bathing pan. When *Baba* dipped his feet into the water she scrubbed them making sure that all the dirt was loosened and washed away from between the toes. Satisfied that they were clean, she would take up the towel and rub each foot till it was comfortably dry. Of course, when Govind was five years old, he took over the duty of washing *Baba's* feet. It was but natural that *Baba* would prefer the attention of his son.

When *Baba* no longer needed her, Vashti was free

for other duties. Meenu was two years old then and it was easy to see that she would never be like other children. While Mama crouched on the floor and coaxed dung chips to burn in the *chula* (stove), Vashti played with Meenu to keep her out of *Baba's* sight.

Poor Meenu! Vashti loved her but she knew little sister would be better off if she had never drawn the breath of life. She was born in the year of the Big Drought. Vashti remembered the year and how her parents scanned the skies each night hoping for signs of rain. The heavens were beautiful, the stars hung close to the earth but the clouds they hoped to see were never there. The monsoon rains should have started weeks before. *Baba* watched the water in his rice paddy grow lower and lower until the green shoots turned slimy brown. The millet field withered and died from the red ball of heat. Women could no longer wash the families' clothes. A river bed of cracked brown clay was the only reminder that a chattering stream had once provided water so that they could scrub their garments at the river's edge. The *panchayat*—a group of elders who settle village affairs decided drinking water must be rationed. They dared not run the risk of a dry well.

When the rains finally came the crops of the season were already gone. The downpour brought relief from the burning sun but no one showed any signs of joy. Joy or sorrow, either feeling took effort and none could spare the strength.

Baba had saved seed when they were all but starving knowing it meant their future survival. Now he and the bullock went into the fields to plow and plant. Both were so weak that they could go only a few feet before they stopped to rest.

In the Prakash home, the dried fish, the rice, the millet were gone. There were no garden vegetables to eke out a meal. Vashti wakened from dreams of food to hear her brother whimpering in his sleep. While they waited for the second crop to grow, Mama dug edible roots and boiled them. She forced out the soft pulp of the prickly pear and doled it out. Plantain leaves could be eaten without ill effects. She stripped the leaves from the plants as they appeared.

When all the seeds were in, *Baba* would leave the house early every morning and walk the country road to the town of Savonkota six miles away. There he delved into the garbage thrown out by well-to-do families and carried home anything that his own family might eat. Once he caught a dog as it crept from the roadside to die. He shouldered it and managed to get it to the village. The Hindu religion forbade eating meat but dog filled the pot and then the belly. Mama retched at the unfamiliar smell of meat cooking but she served it up and managed to eat a little herself.

The moneylender sent word for *Baba* to bring the interest to his store. *Baba* went empty-handed.

"I have no money," he said, knowing full well his statement would not soften the marble-hearted man.

"Then get it. You have property. You can give me what you owe," his extortioner answered.

A glance around the store showed *Baba* brass pots and bowls, chairs, harness, even the wedding garments of other unfortunate persons. He could raise no money with such items. Except for his father's chair, he had parted with all personal goods of value long ago. The chair was in poor condition and he had been offered so little for it that he had kept it. Such a piece of furniture

FAITH REFORMED LIBRARY,
ROUTE 3 — BOX 19
KANKAKEE, ILLINOIS 60901

was a reminder that the Prakash family had not always been in such circumstances. With the chair at home to prove he was not an ordinary ragtag, he could do almost anything to provide his family with food.

"If I sell more land, I cannot raise enough grain to feed my family and meet my future payments," *Baba* pointed out to the moneylender.

"That is your problem. I have enough of my own," the miserly man retorted. "I'll be generous. I'll give you a week to raise it."

Baba went home and talked to his wife about the money.

"Maybe your brother will give it to you," Mama suggested.

"We have gone over that before. He claims the jute mills in Bartoor do not run full time and he makes barely enough for them to live on."

"He would surely help his brother if he knew how things are with us," Mama insisted.

"He has done enough. He could have claimed his share of the farm and sold it when our father died. Instead, he let me have it all and he went to find a living somewhere else."

"To have claimed his share of the farm would have meant claiming his share of your *Baba's* debt. He was wise to hand the land and debt over to you," Mama said.

"I could not walk to Bartoor and return within a week, anyway," *Baba* told her. "Tomorrow, I'll sell my bullock."

"The *rupees* you receive for the bullock will not pay the interest," Mama said.

"True, but they will help."

Both of them knew another piece of farm must go.

Baba could never have walked to Bartoor and home again. He was too weak. With so little to eat, all of them were listless. They stayed inside the house in the heat of the day as much as it was possible. Mama was especially listless although she planted her garden and tended it while Vashti looked after little Govind.

One day the neighbor's child, who was ten years old, sat with Vashti and Govind in the shade of the house while Mama hoed the lentils.

"Your mama will have a baby," the ten-year-old said.

"How do you know?" Vashti asked.

"Because her belly is big."

Vashti had looked first at her own middle and then at the girl's beside her. Although their arms and legs were like sticks, their abdomens were swollen with air.

"Are we going to have babies?" she asked.

"No, stupid. Only mamas have them," her informant replied.

If Mama was going to have a little baby, Vashti thought she would be glad. She wasn't. Vashti had never seen her when she seemed more unhappy. Was it because *Baba* whispered angrily to her when they lay on their mats at night? Vashti had heard him mutter the words, "Another mouth." But a baby would cost them nothing in food. It would draw milk from Mama's breast.

One evening at suppertime, Mama did not look well. She served the family and then unrolled her mat and lay down.

When they had eaten, *Baba* said to Govind, "You will go next door for the night." He turned to Vashti.

"Hurry and wash. We will get Mrs. Baksh."

Vashti dutifully washed herself and then reached for one of *Baba's* hands as they started to walk to the other end of the village.

"Why are we going for Mrs. Baksh?" she asked.

"Your mama needs a midwife," *Baba* answered.

Vashti didn't know what a midwife was but she thought *Baba* might be angry if she asked more questions so she walked on in silence.

Mrs. Baksh appeared to be waiting for the summons to the Prakash home. She picked up a little bag and left with them immediately.

"Do not give it the slap. It must not draw breath," *Baba* ordered her.

"I must," she told him. "If I withheld life I would bring bad luck to the whole village," the midwife answered.

Baba stopped as if to send the woman home again. Reluctantly, he moved forward again.

"Perhaps the child will be born dead. It is my wish that it does not live. But do what you must do. Only be sure my Gauri lives," he said.

Vashti and *Baba* sat outside the house and the midwife went in to Mama. They sat there a long while. Vashti leaned her head against her father and went to sleep. She was aroused as *Baba* stirred. She heard a faint cry within. After another interval Mrs. Baksh came out.

"It is a girl and she lives," she said as she started homeward.

Baba went inside. He didn't speak to Mama or look at the child. He lay down to sleep.

Mama tried to get up next morning but she was too

40

weak. Vashti went to the *chula* and blew on the embers to bring them alive, but she did not have enough breath. *Baba* helped her and the coals warmed the chips and brought them to a flame.

They had eaten plantain leaves the night before. Now Vashti did as she had seen her mother do. She warmed the water in which the leaves had been cooked. Each person had a portion for breakfast.

When *Baba* had drunk his share, he walked over to the mat where his wife lay. "When you are able to walk you must drown it in the river."

"No." Mama's voice was weak but determined.

"I said you must. Better that it should die now than live to starve," *Baba* said.

"She has as much right to live as you or I have," Mama declared.

The argument went on for weeks. *Baba* may have seen that Mama would never give in and he could not bring himself to drown a child. Or perhaps when he saw the grain heads fill out and knew that a full stomach was in sight he grew more optimistic. At any rate, he said no more.

When Vashti looked at Meenu for the first time, she thought she looked like a wizened old woman, wrapped in rags. As food became more plentiful, the layers of skin filled out and she became a beautiful baby. But early in her life, Meenu showed signs of being dull-witted. Mama gave her a great deal of attention. She wanted her to notice and do things that Vashti and Govind had done as babies. It was no use. Meenu would never grow mentally as she should.

"It is my fault," Mama said as though speaking to herself. "When she was within me, I did not give her

41

food good enough to make her brain right."

Poor Meenu! Poor Mama! For she still blamed herself.

"Vashti!" It was Mrs. Ghose speaking to her. "It is time we go to the barn for milking. Did you not hear me calling?"

Vashti shook her head.

"Come. You can talk to the buffaloes awhile and then go to supper. You are hungry, aren't you?" Mrs. Ghose asked.

"No," Vashti answered. "I am not used to eating three meals a day."

"You will find it a habit that grows on you," the woman answered jokingly. "Now tell me, what fills your pretty head that I must call you three times to tell you it is time to quit work? Were you dreaming of a handsome man who will be your husband some day?"

Vashti blushed. "Nothing like that." She thought Mrs. Ghose was the kind of person she might be able to talk to, but not yet. She told her none of the thoughts that filled her mind while she hoed up and down the rows of corn.

4

The Christian
Brotherhood of Sharing

"Where do you live?" Radha asked Vashti.

It was study period but the two girls wanted time to know one another better. They sat on the mat between their two cots in the hostel, their feet flat on the floor, their knees drawn up even with their chins.

"Calcutta," Vashti answered.

"How did you get here?" Radha asked.

"In a motorcar." Vashti's eyes sparkled remembering the ride from the city. "I came with Miss Narain. We went so fast we seemed to be flying. It was exciting."

"I take the bus when I come here. It goes fast, too," Radha said.

"Where do you live?" Vashti asked now.

"In Chandpur. It is a big town but not a city like Calcutta. Most of the people in my father's church are very poor but he has raised them up from their low place in life. Some were untouchables, but there is no caste in Christianity."

"No caste?" Vashti said, surprised.

"Well, actually there isn't supposed to be caste in India anymore. The government made a law that says so," Radha explained.

"How can they make such a law when the Hindu law says we belong in castes?"

Radha shrugged.

"When the untouchables become Christians does everyone treat them as if they are no longer untouchable?" Vashti inquired.

"Those of Hindu faith still treat them as *outcastes*. If their shadow should fall upon a Brahman or Kshatriya, that person feels himself unclean and goes home and bathes."

"Of course," said Vashti. "He has been taught to do so."

"Yet Brahmans who have become Christians sit at the table in my father's house and eat with untouchables," Radha said.

Vashti showed great surprise. "I wouldn't want to eat with an untouchable. I know Christian people are good. They pay a lot of money so I can go to school here. But it is a strange religion. I could never be a Christian," she declared.

"I know how you feel. My father and mother were of the Hindu faith and *Baba* says it takes a long while to change to Christianity. The religions are very different even though both believe in one Supreme Being."

"My family worships the goddess Lakshmi," Vashti stated.

"Please forgive me for saying this, but one of the greatest wrongs in the Hindu religion is all the gods and goddesses that have been added to it. They are only symbols and yet people forget the Great Creator and put their trust in stone images," Radha said.

"Don't you have gods and goddesses?" Vashti asked.

"We believe in one God who is the Creator of Heaven and earth. God sent His Son, Jesus Christ, to us as a little baby. Jesus grew up and taught people how to live in a way that was pleasing to the Father in Heaven. But God says, 'You shall have no other gods before me.' "

Vashti didn't like the way the conversation was going. It was plain that she would never have help from Radha in finding an image of Lakshmi to worship. She reached for her books. "I must study my lessons," she said.

Radha picked up her books, too, and the two girls studied until lights were turned off.

As they lay on their cots side by side, Radha said, "You aren't angry at me, are you?"

"No," Vashti answered.

"Tell me what Calcutta is like. I've never been in a big city."

"It is horrible. There are people everywhere. They live in huts and some live on the sidewalk so you have to walk in the street. People die and they are left where they lay until the truck picks them up in the morning. I don't like to talk about it," Vashti said and shuddered.

"I had no idea it was like that. When Miss Narain

45

comes, she looks so clean and healthy. Surely all Calcutta isn't the way you say."

"No. After Miss Narain stopped for me she drove through clean streets where there were nice homes. She took me to her house and it was lovely. She had a bathroom and it was pink and white with a tub big enough to lie down in. It was like being in another world."

Suddenly, a voice came out of the darkness. "Will you girls quit talking so we can go to sleep?" It was Purnima's scolding voice.

"We'll be quiet," Radha said. "Good night Vashti," she whispered.

"Good night," Vashti answered.

Vashti wished Radha hadn't asked her about Calcutta. It brought back awful memories of the *bustee*. Besides, now at least one of the girls would have a pretty good idea what her family home was like. For two days now she had lived at this clean school and hostel where she had plenty of nourishing food and a well-ordered life of work, study, and classes. But those she loved still lived on the oddments Mama could buy from her pay and Govind's begging money. They still dodged the rich man's motorcars in the street, stepped into the filth of the gutters, and endured the stench of human excrement because there was no way of getting away from it.

She tried to escape such thoughts by going back to the family life they lived when they were in the village of Bajribasha. There had been pleasant years after Meenu's birth. The rice and millet crops were good and *Baba* could sell enough to pay interest to the moneylender. To their joy, if they skimped a little themselves, there would be enough to buy barley seed so that their land could give them two crops, barley planted in late fall and millet and rice planted in July.

With the extra money from the barley, *Baba* replaced the bullock he had been forced to sell in the Big Drought. Then he no longer needed to pull the plow while Mama guided it.

The year after the bullock found its place in their small courtyard, *Baba* bought a goat. Now he looked upon Meenu with favor.

Smacking his lips between mouthfuls of curds made from goat's milk, he said, "Gauri, you were right to keep the child. The *bewakoof* (idiot) has brought us good fortune."

Vashti remembered Mama's sweet smile. *Baba's* late approval more than made up for his anger when she had refused to drown Meenu in the river.

And there was the joy of learning. Of course, it was Govind who went to school but Vashti studied more diligently than Govind did. Her brother had a quick mind and he could pass his grades without working very hard. But Vashti wanted to know everything that was written in the books and she didn't miss a word that was there. The government had little paper to give its students so there was barely enough for Govind's work. Using a stick, Vashti solved her arithmetic problems on the hard ground. The mud walls of their home were as solid as a blackboard. Vashti kept a supply of limestone to use as chalk and she practiced her writing on the outside surface of their house.

But good times came to an end. There were two years of drought, one following the other. They were forced from their home and eventually they became one more family among the millions who made up the *bustee* of Calcutta.

But not right away. First there was the long period of searching the sky for the rain clouds. Then they watched the stove-like heat of the sun dry up the garden, burn the millet in the field, and lift a portion of water daily from the rice paddy until there was no hope for a crop.

Again the Prakash family lived on roots, on boiled leaves, on garbage from the more prosperous people who lived in Savonkota. But *Baba* remembered the school principal predicting that an education might mean as much as 700 extra *rupees* when marriage arrangements were being made for his son.

"Your brother must keep up his strength. He must walk six miles to school. Must you eat so much?" he would ask Vashti.

Reluctantly, she let Govind take a bite or two from her bowl but she thought it unfair. Wasn't it enough that her father let her brother go to school? Must he also have the food she needed so badly herself?

Baba plainly begrudged the food that went into Meenu's mouth, but when he took from her and gave to Govind he saw his wife shared her portion with the child. Gauri was necessary to the household. If she should die how then could he care for this family and plant his fields? When the rains came and the season was right, she must guide the plow while he would pull it. Again their bullock and their goat, too, had gone to pay interest on the loan. The money-lender claimed four *guntha* (acres) of farmland as well.

Govind finished the school term that first year of drought though he might not have made it had it not

48

been for one of his Savonkota classmates. The boy shared his lunch with him and in return Govind worked his problems each day.

Baba hadn't much hope for the barley crop but he put it in when planting time came. Although the heads were not well-filled out, still he harvested a little. And Mama grew a few vegetables and a good amount of mustard seed. She could press out the mustard oil and cook with it, then add the crushed seeds to flavor anything she found to cook.

Baba made no attempt to hold back part of the barley to pay interest to the moneylender. He seemed very despondent.

"Let us eat as long as there is food. We have not enough to exist on as it is," he said.

"What will we do when the moneylender makes his demands?" Mama asked.

Baba raised his voice and shouted so loud Meenu began to cry. "Is it not enough that I know I am a ruined man?" he said. "Must you make me put it into words? The moneylender will take all that I have when he comes again."

Day in, day out, he sat inside the house, the image of gloom. The family learned to walk with care lest they arouse his anger.

When July came and he made no move to leave the house, Mama said, "It is time to prepare the rice paddy. Should we not be at work there?"

"There can be no rice planting. The river is too low to flood the land," he answered.

Mama trembled realizing how precarious life could be when one must depend on the whims of the gods to send rain and sun. She soaked a little of the rice they had kept as seed. When it was fully swollen so it would require little cooking, she brought it to a boil using a few cow chips in the *chula*. Even cow dung had become precious. The cattle found little to graze upon and so had little waste. At night, their constant hunger-bawling kept everyone in the village awake.

"What are you cooking in the middle of the day?" *Baba* asked.

"Rice. We must make a sacramental offering to Lakshmi," Mama replied. "Perhaps she is displeased with us and that is why she will not interfere in our behalf."

"Gauri, you are as much a *bewakoof* as your child Meenu. Does not the sun shine on the fields of others the same as ours? And have they not made sacrifice to the gods and goddesses? But go. One more offering cannot bring us further disaster and it might do good."

Mama hurried from the house and prayed long when she laid her offering at the altar of Lakshmi.

When she returned home she said, "We can plow and sow the millet field. It requires no flooding and rain may yet fall to sprout the seeds."

"We'll sow no millet. With all the land that has been taken from us, we cannot live on our plot and meet interest payments; no matter how good the crop. At harvest time the moneylender will come and make further claim. Let us not leave a field of millet for him to reap."

Baba no longer appeared interested in anything about his land or home. Mama cooked roots and weeds adding a little rice or barley or millet for their evening meal. She winced each time she dipped into the grain that had been held back for seed. But they must eat one meal a day if they were to survive. For breakfast, they drank the water that their supper had been cooked in.

Although he was quick to learn, Govind was not interested in getting an education. He often skipped school. *Baba* did not appear to notice when he stayed home and Govind capitalized upon his father's disinterest by dropping school entirely. He had not returned his textbooks and Vashti spent all her time studying when she was free from work.

One day when Mama and Vashti were in the yard loosening the dirt around the pumpkin vines (Gauri had not given up the idea of growing food), Govind ran through the yard as if a *churail* (evil spirit) were after him.

"Govind, where are you going? What's wrong?" Mama asked.

"I'm hiding. Teacher is coming and I'm not going back to that school," he said as he kept on running.

Presently a pleasant young lady came into the yard.

Mrs. Prakash wiped the soil from her hands on the hem of her *sari* (dress worn by Indian women) and went to meet her.

"I am Miss Narain, one of Govind's teachers," the young lady said.

Mama saw how new and pretty the teacher's clothes were, how neat and shapely her feet. She dropped her eyes, embarrassed at her own appearance before this grand lady.

"I am Govind's mother," she murmured.

"He is not coming to school and yet he must be keeping up his lessons. I could not help noticing the writing that covers the walls of your house. I can see it is from fourth grade books."

"Govind doesn't like to go to school and Mr. Prakash no longer cares," Mama answered.

"But surely, if he keeps up his studies—and I can see that he does—" She looked puzzled. "What is it about school he doesn't like?"

"Govind did not put the words on our walls. It was my daughter." She indicated Vashti who stood a few steps behind her.

When Miss Narain focused her attention on Vashti the girl looked down at her feet, digging her toes into the sun-baked dirt.

"Do you go to school?" Miss Narain asked.

"No, Miss." Vashti's answer was almost a whisper.

"She studies her brother's books," Mrs. Prakash said.

"Would you like to go to school?" Miss Narain asked.

Vashti's face glowed like a lighted candle. "Oh, yes."

"There is an organization, the Christian Brotherhood of Sharing. I might be able to arrange it through them," Miss Narain said. "Of course, it would mean leaving your family."

"I don't know if my husband would let her go to school. A girl has no need for books," Mama said.

Miss Narain wondered how Govind could care so little for learning when he had a sister who cared so much. She watched Vashti now. Malnutrition was evident. Her eyes were set in deep hollows , yet the yearning she saw was for knowledge, not food.

"I don't work for the Brotherhood but I have a good friend there. Let me talk to her and try to arrange it. There is time enough after that to approach Mr. Prakash," Miss Narain said.

When she had ascertained that she would have no help from the family in getting Govind back in the classroom, she went away.

Everything happened as *Baba* said it would. The moneylender took the acre of land that remained of the farm and he claimed their house in the village as well. It was legal. Until this year, interest had been kept up, but no money had ever been paid on the loan made to *Tata* so long ago. It seemed to all of them that the moneylender exulted when he picked up *Tata's* chair and carried it away to his store.

The family was crushed. Everything known to them was swept away and the future was black to say the least. But Vashti was desolated. She felt she had lost her chance of ever getting an education. If Miss Narain should be successful in getting her into a school, she would seek her out in the village and the Prakash family would be gone. The realization was bitter to her tongue.

The rains came but, of course, they came too late. The downpour drenched *Baba,* Gauri, Vashti, Govind and Meenu as they walked away from the village. It soaked the meager belongings they carried with them. Their bare feet squished in the mud or plopped hollowly when they pulled them from especially deep mire.

Within a week, they hoped to reach Bartoor where *Baba's* brother lived. They had nowhere else to go.

5

The Failed Test

Vashti found chapel at the mission school as interesting as the classes she loved so much. Her enjoyment was accompanied by a feeling of guilt because she knew *Baba* would make a great fuss if he knew she listened to stories of the Christian God and His Son. She tried to relieve her conscience by telling herself that chapel was just like a school subject to her, a subject that all students must take. After Miss Narain had talked to *Baba,* he wanted her to get an education so she could better the lot of the Prakash family.

The singing at chapel bothered her at first. She could not attune her ear or voice to the Christian hymns.

"Why does the singing sound so different?" she asked Shoba one evening as they were walking down to the milking shed. Shoba was a little older than Vashti but very friendly.

"The missionaries come from the West and teach their hymns as they sing them in Europe. Maybe that is how the Christian God likes to hear the songs," Shoba answered.

"Are you Christian?" Vashti asked.

"No. I'm Hindu."

"So am I," Vashti answered, glad that she had at last found someone of her own faith. "Is Lakshmi your family goddess?"

"No. We worship Mitra."

"Do you know where I can find a shrine to Lakshmi? She is our family goddess," Vashti said.

"I don't but you can go with me to worship Mitra if you like. We have time to ourselves on Sunday afternoon and I go then," Shoba told her.

Vashti knew she would feel freer to make her supplications to Lakshmi who seemed like a long-time friend but it was better to pray to Mitra than not to pray at all. "I'll go. Thank you."

One of the things Vashti liked most about chapel were stories Miss Adhikari told the girls. Most of them were about Jesus and they often showed His great compassion for the poor and sick. One morning she told how the Master (that was what Miss Adhikari called Him) laid His hands upon a leper and healed the man through His miraculous power.

Vashti knew about lepers. She had seen them on the streets of Calcutta. She learned that the city tried to keep all lepers in a colony by themselves outside the

56

city because they thought the disease was very contagious. It would be a terrible thing to live away from loved ones and not know if they were sick or well, if their children had food or were hungry.

Vashti thought it was wonderful that Jesus would lay His hands upon the leper and say, "You are healed." Jesus had not been concerned that the man was repulsive to look at. Perhaps He had put His hand down on the white mottled flesh where a sore was breaking through. And He had said very simply, "You are healed."

The leper must have been beside himself with joy when he saw that he was well and could go home to his people again. If he had a family he would be able to support them if he could find a job.

Vashti determined to pray that Mama should be rid of her cough when she went with Shoba to Mitra's temple on Sunday. It should be much easier to make her mother well than it would be to cure a leper.

In the hostel she caught herself looking at Radha's picture of the Master pinned to the wall. When Radha first put up the picture Vashti had thought Jesus would be a kind man. Now, after listening to Miss Adhikari's stories, He seemed more kindly than ever. She could almost imagine He was living today, that He was someone she knew.

On Sunday, Shoba and Vashti left the hostel to walk to Lorabad where the Mitra temple stood.

"Did you hold back some of your rice from dinner?" Shoba asked.

"Do you mean for an offering?" Vashti asked. "No. I wasn't sure the school would want me to."

"Never mind. I took plenty from my bowl and I'll

divide with you," Shoba told her.

When they came to the temple, she poured rice into the extra leaf she had brought and handed it to Vashti. The two girls approached the sculptured image.

Again Vashti wished it were Lakshmi she worshiped. But she bowed her head until it touched the cool cement of the floor and she prayed for the well-being of each member of her family. After that, she made a special petition for her mother, praying that she would be rid of her cough. "If I don't ask too much, will the great god Mitra please keep her from bleeding?" she pleaded. She repeated her prayer several times. When she rose from her cramped position she flexed her neck to loosen the stiffness. She had grown tense in her effort to reach the god Mitra.

Shoba had made her homage and she waited for Vashti near the street. The two girls talked little as they walked back to the hostel.

Before Vashti went to bed that evening, she looked again at Radha's picture of Jesus. Her trip to the shrine had given her no feeling of fulfillment. Mitra seemed a strange god to her. It would take several trips to the temple, probably, before she felt she had reached him.

Shantha had predicted well when she told Vashti she would probably be moved out of fifth grade into sixth grade "mats" soon.

One day Miss Dal, the teacher, asked her to remain after class. "Your work shows you are beyond the other students. Would you like to try sixth grade work?" she asked.

Vashti warmed with pleasure. "Yes, I would."

"As you know, I teach sixth grade, too. If you have trouble with the problems, I'll give you outside help,"

58

Miss Dal said. "Would you like to take the book with you now?"

As Vashti strolled along clutching her new book she met Shantha.

When her friend saw the book she carried, she said, "Are you going to be in my mats class?"

"Yes," Vashti said happily.

Shantha was delighted. "I'll help you if you need any help catching up," she said.

One person showed no enthusiasm for Vashti's promotion and that was Purnima. Vashti had made her look foolish before the other girls and she hadn't forgiven her. She had begun to plan a way to get back at her.

Like most of the girls, Purnima worked to pay for part of her schooling. She had been assigned one classroom to clean each day. Now she asked that she might change the room she cleaned for Miss Dal's room.

"Why do you want to make the change?" Miss Adhikari asked.

"No special reason, but it gets tiresome cleaning the same room all the time," Purnima answered, assuming a look of candor.

"I suppose it can be arranged. I'm sure the girl assigned to clean that room wouldn't mind trading. I want all my students to be happy doing their work," the principal said.

"You're very kind, Miss Adhikari. And I'm sure I'll be happier sweeping Miss Dal's room than doing the one I have now."

Purnima wore a look of innocence that hid any sign of the plot she was hatching up to discredit Vashti. She knew her plan would require patience but someday the opportunity would come for her to put it into action.

Meanwhile, Vashti's future looked brighter every day. She had been promoted to sixth grade in grammar and spelling, too. She put in as much time as possible studying the English language knowing that she would be studying English textbooks in eighth grade. Radha was a great help to her here. Her mother was half English and spoke the language as well as she spoke Hindi. Knowing how helpful English was to any Indian child, she taught Radha to speak it before she was five years old.

Another of Vashti's achievements was overcoming her fear of the buffaloes and taking her turn at milking them. When she had followed Mrs. Ghose to the milk shed a few times, the woman suggested that she begin stroking the buffalo.

"You mean while you are milking?" Vashti asked.

Mrs. Ghose nodded.

"But it might be afraid and kick you," the girl said.

"I don't think so. It is too big to be afraid of a little one like you," Mrs. Ghose answered.

Cautiously, Vashti reached out her hand until her fingertips touched the buffalo's side. Nothing happened which was reassuring so she brought her hand down across the animal's side. She jumped back when the buffalo gave her a curious look. When there was no other reaction, she gained courage and stroked it once more.

When milking was finished, Mrs. Ghose walked to the animal's head, slapped it on its neck and fed it a handful of hay from her hand. "Come on," she encouraged Vashti. "Let it have food from your own hand. Then the buffalo will know you are not afraid and it will like you."

Vashti wasn't sure she could fool the animal because she really was afraid. Keeping as far distant as possible, she held out a handful of hay and the buffalo took it unconcernedly and gave it a proper munching.

Two nights later she took Mrs. Ghose's place squatting almost under the *arna*. She pulled on its teats and sent a stream of milk into the vessel. She felt good doing the task. She liked the animal scent of the *arna's* body and the warm milk odor as it came forth in a stream.

Shortly after Vashti began milking, Miss Adhikari added another buffalo to the household. Three, she explained, did not supply enough milk to provide the proper diet to her family of 300 schoolgirls.

The cloud that still hovered was the need Vashti felt for her family. Miss Narain had given her some postage stamps and she had written to the address where it was arranged her brother would call for her letters. He would be able to read them to her mother and father. If he had received the letters, he had not written in return. Vashti worried about Mama and Meenu. She hoped *Baba* no longer struck them when he was angry.

Parents of the girls who were living at the hostel were allowed to come once each month to visit their daughters. Many of the parents could not come because the distance was too great to walk and they hadn't the money to take a bus. But Vashti found a homesick lump lodged in her throat every time she saw any of the girls run out and embrace their mother and father.

Examination time came and Vashti felt confident that she had done well in all her tests. This in spite of the fact that she had been moved to a higher grade in some of them. Her high spirits were soon dashed. Miss Dal passed out the arithmetic papers as the girls came into the room. Vashti had failed miserably. It seemed impossible that her grade could be as bad as it was.

Miss Dal used the class period to go over the test and explain the problems. Vashti scarcely heard her. She sat and stared at the failing grade as if she were stunned. Would she be put back in the fifth grade? she wondered.

Miss Dal stopped her when class was over and the girls were leaving.

"I thought you were doing very well in sixth," she said. "Your papers and class work have been good. What happened to you when you took the test?"

Vashti felt her eyes go wet. She looked down so Miss Dal would not notice. "I thought I did well," she said.

"I told you to come to me if you needed help. You didn't come. I can only say again, please seek me out when you don't understand how to work the problems," Miss Dal told her. "You may be excused."

Vashti headed for the hostel, crushed by her failure but thankful, at least, that Miss Dal hadn't put her back in fifth. It was lunch time but she felt too badly to eat. She lay down on the mat beside her cot and wept.

She and Radha usually ate together and her friend had missed her. Radha asked several girls if they had seen her but none of them had. She went to the hostel looking for her.

When Vashti heard her coming she forced herself to quit crying and wiped away the tears.

"Here you are," Radha exclaimed. "I've been looking for you. Why didn't you come to lunch?"

"I wasn't hungry," Vashti answered.

"You've been crying," Radha said. "What's the matter?"

"I failed in mats. I'm silly to cry. It isn't important."

"It is important!" Radha exclaimed. "You thought you did so well in mats. What happened?"

"I don't know. I couldn't bear to look at my paper. I saw my grade and I didn't want to see any more," Vashti said, near tears again.

"Come on. Pick up your courage. Let's look at the problems," Radha said.

Vashti opened the paper and she and Radha began reading it together.

"That's not the answer I put down," Vashti cried, looking at the first problem.

"Look! It's been erased. Whoever did it did a good job but you can see the erasure marks," Radha said.

"But I didn't erase any of my answers," Vashti exclaimed.

"And this one's been erased and this one's been erased!" Radha declared. "Someone has done some dirty work and I can guess who."

"Purnima! She cleans the room. But how did she get the chance? Miss Dal wouldn't leave our test papers lying around," Vashti said.

"Maybe she went out and something kept her longer than she expected to be. If Purnima meant to do this she would have been waiting for such a chance," Radha said.

"I'm afraid you're right. She's never liked me because I corrected her mats problem when I first came.

"She should have thanked you for showing her the mistake," Radha said.

"But I didn't need to point it out in front of all you girls. And now she has hurt me but she's hurt herself more. I'm the one who's really to blame," Vashti said regretfully.

"You're to blame!" Radha sounded exasperated. "Don't be so humble. She's a mean girl and she picked the nastiest way she knew to do you harm."

"But don't you see what she has done to herself? This will be held against her when she is reborn," Vashti explained.

Radha's patience was at an end. "I give up. I'll never understand the attitude of you Hindus. Besides, you know we Christians don't believe in reincarnation. I'm leaving for class." She picked up her books and Vashti followed her downstairs.

But Radha didn't drop the subject of the altered test papers. She told several of the girls and they agreed that Purnima was responsible. When Purnima came upstairs after the evening meal, Shantha confronted her.

"You changed the answers on Vashti's test paper, didn't you?" she demanded.

"I don't know what you're talking about and Vashti's got no right to accuse me. If she failed, it's because she's not smart enough to do sixth grade work," Purnima answered, walking over to her own cot and sitting down.

Shoba and Lata walked over and stood one on each side of the bed. "Admit it!" they said.

"I didn't do anything. I didn't do it!" Purnima declared shrilly.

Shoba and Lata pushed her shoulders down on the cot, then Shoba took hold of her hand. "Do you want me to break your arm?" she asked.

Vashti started toward the girls but Purnima confessed before she could stop them.

"Don't hurt me. I'll tell the truth. I did it," she said, starting to cry.

"Please let go of her," Vashti said to Shoba.

But Shoba kept hold of Purnima's hand. "Why?" she demanded.

"Because she thinks she's so smart and she's not as smart as I am or she wouldn't be partly in fifth grade," Purnima answered.

"Make her promise to go to Miss Dal and tell her," Shantha said.

"No, don't make her do that. I don't want to put her to shame. I'll ask Miss Dal if she will let me take another test," Vashti told the girls. Then she turned to Purnima. "But if you do it again I'll tell Miss Dal myself."

The girls in the room had their own way of punishing Purnima. They ignored her. She asked to be transferred to another room at the hostel but Miss Adhikari would not make the change. When her other classmates heard what she had done, they too gave her the silent treatment.

Shortly after the episode of the altered test paper, October vacation arrived. Purnima welcomed the chance to leave the school. She hoped the girls would forget by the time they were back in November.

Vashti did not look forward to vacation. She hadn't the means of getting home and she thought she would spend a month of lonely days.

6

Vacation and Mrs. Ghose

Vashti kept herself so busy during the October vacation that she had no time to be lonely.

The teachers had left the school but Mrs. Ghose came every day and Vashti spent the time working with her in the garden.

"Miss Adhikari gives the girls a vacation but the weeds won't take one. Not a minute of time do they rest from growing. So we fight them each day as always," Mrs. Ghose said.

Vashti didn't mind the "fight." In the morning the dew on the grass blades sparkled like the gems she had seen on the fingers of wealthy ladies in Calcutta. Such foolish ladies! They traveled through the *bustee* in taxis or in their own motorcars, their hands lying care-lessly across the car door, while people of the street staggered from hunger. It was not unthinkable that a man should ignore the horn's honking and leap to the side of the automobile to tear the rings from a soft, well-shaped hand. Such a picture came vividly to Vashti. At times, she could even believe a desperate starveling would chop off a finger to take his prize.

But these people were far removed from Vashti as she kept up the rhythmical rise and fall of the hoe, clearing the way for the garden stuff to grow at its best. Vashti had a certain sense of wonder about green things growing. She loved to watch sprouts push through the dark earth, not yet green but tender white. It was the yellow rays of sun that changed their color but they owed part of their growth to her as she tended and watered the plants.

Not all her day was spent in the garden. Miss Adhikari had taken the sting of homesickness from her when she suggested that the month of October would be a good time for her to study ahead of the class.

"I've had good reports from all your teachers," she said. "Perhaps by the time classes reopen in November you will be qualified to do sixth grade work in all your studies."

With such encouragement, Vashti was willing to put in every minute possible poring over her books. She could not ignore the other girls who, like herself, were not able to go home for the holiday. She thought they might be as lonely as she had expected to be. She stayed and talked each afternoon when the noontime meal had been eaten.

She came to feel a natural affection for Mrs. Ghose.

It was as if the gardener was a dear aunt or some other close relative. Not often but sometimes she remembered Miss Adhikari had said Mrs. Ghose was a Dravidian. What had she meant? How was her friend different from herself or, perhaps, Radha? Vashti still entertained the thought that the black woman might be a sorceress but it no longer troubled her. If she had powers of magic, Vashti was sure her powers were for good. How could a person who made everyone around her feel good have evil within her?

One evening as the two of them were walking toward the milk shed where they shared the task of milking the four *arnas,* Mrs. Ghose said, "My little helper wears firm flesh where once the skin covered only bones."

"It is because the school feeds us well," Vashti answered.

"You did not eat well before you came to school?" Mrs. Ghose asked sorrowfully.

"We did when we lived in the village and *Baba* grew good crops. That seems a long while ago," she said meditatively.

"Why did you leave the village?" Mrs. Ghose inquired.

"We owed a debt to the moneylender. When there was no money *Baba* was forced to give the man a little of the land. When the last drought came he took everything," Vashti explained.

Mrs. Ghose shook her head sadly. Too many times she had heard the story of a moneylender who had sapped the strength and then the soul of a man, leaving him a walking nothing. "And then you went to Calcutta?"

"Not right away. We went to my Uncle Mangal's in

Bartoor first," Vashti explained. "It was a long way and Mama began to cough along the way."

Tears welled up in Vashti's eyes. She could not talk without crying. She placed the vessel under the buffalo and aimed a stream of milk into it. Mrs. Ghose touched her comfortingly and then went on to her own buffalo.

If there had been enough food to give them strength as the rain poured down and they sloshed their way to Uncle Mangal's perhaps Mama would not have yielded to the sickness. Vashti knew the cough was more than a cough. It was tuberculosis. Unless her mother left the *bustee* and had plenty of fresh air and good food, she could not live many years. These were things she had learned from Radha's health book. What chance had Mama to get out of the slums? None.

Drawing the last milk from the *arna's* udder, Vashti set her filled vessel alongside Mrs. Ghose's and moved to the other buffalo she must milk.

Mrs. Ghose walked beside her companionably. "Your uncle, you could not stay with him in Bartoor?" she asked. Her heart had been touched the first time she saw Vashti. The skin drawn tightly across the cheekbones, the eyes set deep into her head told of a starvation diet. Half the souls in India had barely enough food to stay alive, yet Vashti had stirred her sympathy as no one else had done.

"No, we couldn't stay. Uncle Mangal shared what he had with us until he had no work. That was when we went to Calcutta."

It had taken six days to reach Bartoor where Uncle Mangal lived and Uncle had made a poor show of welcome when the bedraggled five met him where he worked. Six days of plodding wearily south.

Before leaving the village Mama had made cakes of most of the rice, millet and barley that remained. She carried it in a bag made from a worn-out *sari* since the moneylender had claimed their cooking vessels. For three days the rain beat down and the hard cakes were softened to mush. Their food had soured by the third day but they dared not waste it. After it was eaten, Mama and Meenu suffered with cramps and all of them had diarrhea. Luckily, on the fourth day the sun came out. Seeing a house along the way, Mama had gone to the door and asked for the use of a cooking vessel and a lighted *spill* (splinter). The woman of the house was a kindly person and supplied Mama with her needs. They built a fire with dung they had picked up along the way and Mama cooked fresh gruel.

Baba didn't know the name of the street where his brother lived. They had never corresponded because neither one could write. But he knew the name of the factory where Mangal worked.

After reaching Bartoor, he inquired along the way until they came to the building. A man with a club guarded the gate.

"No beggars allowed inside the fence," he said loudly as the family approached.

"We do not beg. My brother works here and I've come to see him," *Baba* said.

"What is his name?" the guard asked.

"Mangal Prakash."

"He is inside. He will be out at six o'clock."

The five of them squatted near the fence under a eucalyptus tree.

"You can't wait here. Move on!" the guard shouted.

They walked a few feet away and sat down again but

there was no other tree to give them shade.

"He only wanted to show his authority," *Baba* said. They sweated under the midafternoon sun. Vashti's throat was parched.

At six o'clock, *Baba* went back to the gate. The rest of them stayed where they were.

He watched each man leaving. At last he stepped forward. "Mangal!"

His brother stopped and looked at him quizzically. "Is it Kripal?"

"Of course. Don't you know your own brother?" *Baba* asked.

"It's been 12 years. You are an old man," Mangal said.

"The gods have not been good to me. For two years we have had famine. I'm sorry to thrust ourselves on you but we have no place else to go," *Baba* explained.

"You mean all of you are here? How many?" he asked apprehensively.

"My wife, my son, Govind, my two daughters," *Baba* told him.

"Five extra mouths when I can barely feed my own brood," Mangal said irritably. "But come. Where are the others? One must do what one must do."

Baba indicated the family and they started down the street, the two brothers leading, the others trailing behind.

Working in a factory and drawing a regular wage, *Baba* had expected his brother to live much better than the Prakashes had lived in the village. He found this was not so. The one-room house was built of wooden boxes and other odds and ends. The roof was thatched.

The room was filled when they entered it. Mangal's

wife, carrying a baby on her hip, put more rice to cook when she saw the relatives her husband had brought home. Vashti saw four other children who must be her cousins. The oldest one could be no more than eight years old.

Baba, seeing their poverty, became apologetic. "We will not impose on you long. I will find employment and we will have a place of our own."

"I wish you well," Mangal said.

Next morning *Baba* left the house early and did not return until evening but he hadn't found work.

He didn't try for a job at the hemp rope factory. Seeing how poorly his brother lived, he hoped to find something better. But after a week's search, he said to Mangal, "If you spoke for me, maybe you could get me work where you are."

"No chance. The company is laying off men instead of hiring them," Mangal answered.

"Why is that? Surely there is need for rope," *Baba* said.

"Foreigners don't order hemp rope like they used to. They buy from factories at home who make it from fibers they call synthetics," Mangal said.

The strange words bewildered *Baba,* but he understood Mangal when he said his factory was letting men go. If his brother should be laid off, all of the Prakashes would be in the same predicament. He continued to walk the streets. He left the house earlier and returned later but he could find no work.

The blow finally fell. Mangal came in looking very glum one evening.

"The factory will be closed down for awhile," he told his wife.

She stared at him in alarm. "You are not working?"

"If the factory is closed, how can I work?" he asked her gruffly.

"How long will it be closed?" she asked timidly.

"How do I know? It will stay closed until the company gets orders to be filled," he answered.

Later, when *Baba* returned from job hunting and heard Mangal's news, he said, "We must leave you. But where shall we go?" He looked distraught.

"I know of no other relative but Uncle Jogu. He cannot turn you away being Mama's own brother. Besides, he is a man of means. He has a shop in Calcutta," Mangal said.

"How is it you know these things and I, the eldest brother, do not?" *Baba* asked jealously.

"You remember he was fond of me when he visited us in the village. When I left our home in Bajribasha I went to him," Mangal said.

"Why did you not live with him and work in Calcutta?" *Baba* asked.

Mangal hesitated before he answered. "He is not an easy person to live with. But he cannot turn you away, being a near relative," he hastened to add.

"How do I find our Uncle Jogu?" *Baba* asked.

"He sent me a letter once and I kept it. Can any of you read?" Mangal asked.

"My son, Govind, can read and write, too," *Baba* said proudly.

But it was Vashti who copied down the name and number of the street. *Baba* entrusted it to her keeping when they started out once more on their four-day trek to Calcutta.

Vashti was recalled to her present surroundings

when Mrs. Ghose, carrying her milk vessel on her head, stopped at her side.

"Feeling better?" Mrs. Ghose asked.

"I am fine," Vashti answered, aware suddenly that she hadn't even started milking her second *arna*. She squatted under the animal and prepared to do so.

"Why not let me finish up the milking tonight?" Mrs. Ghose asked.

"Please, no. I like to milk," Vashti declared.

"Then I shall go rub down the other beasts," her friend said. But she did not leave at once.

Mrs. Ghose's sympathy for the young girl demanded that she know more about her. It was as if, by knowing, she could share Vashti's hardships and take part of the pain onto herself. Now she said, "When you started out to go to Calcutta, had you a place in mind to stay? I mean, did you have shelter?"

"Yes. We stayed for awhile with my great-uncle Jogu," Vashti said.

They were bewildered when they reached the big city. There were so many streets, so many houses, so many people. Yes, even so many languages. Vashti learned later to identify Bengali, Punjabi, Telegu, Tamil, and, of course, English.

Upon reaching the outskirts, *Baba* began asking in Hindi the direction of the street where Uncle Jogu lived. The men he found who spoke his tongue had never heard of the street or so it would seem, although a few attempted to direct them on their way. They were sent back the way they had come, they were told to go down streets that came to a dead end, they followed a pointing finger that led them to the city's section of large and well-kept homes with flowers on the

76

lawn and bougainvillaea crisscrossing the house walls.

Meenu was fretful and wanted no one but Mama.

"Gauri, put the child down," *Baba* ordered. "We will sit here and rest awhile."

"Does Uncle Jogu live in a house like one of these?" Govind asked.

"Perhaps. Some of these people may be merchants just as he is," *Baba* said.

They did not stay long to rest. A man came out of the house leading a vicious-looking dog.

"Begone or I'll let this beast loose," he said.

The family hurried away.

At last, seeing a policeman, *Baba* overcame his fear of the uniform and went to him for directions. Luckily, the man spoke *Hindi*.

"Your uncle lives a long way from here. The address is in the *bustee*," he said.

"The *bustee*? But he is a man of means. He has his own shop," *Baba* said.

The policeman shrugged. "There are shops in the *bustee*. You cannot reach his place by nightfall unless you take a *jutka* (cab)."

Baba made no reply except to thank the man. As they moved out of earshot *Baba* muttered, "Take a *jutka*. Do I look like a man with money to hire a *jutka*?"

They slept that night near garbage cans behind a bakery shop. Govind lifted the lid of the can and found a few stale *loochi* (fried wheatcakes) the baker had thrown out. He took a huge bite before Mama grabbed them from him. "They must be wiped off," she said.

When she had scraped them she gave each of the family a portion.

Finally they came to Uncle Jogu's shop. It was

midafternoon and they stood off and surveyed it before they made themselves known. It was a sore disappointment. The place should not be called a shop; it was a stall about five feet wide and 12 feet deep with a gate separating it from the street. Behind the gate but out of reach of passersby, were some cheap glass bangles and trinkets of tarnished brass. Hanging from the rafters were a few lengths of material for *saris,* coarse and unattractive. There was little else to be seen.

Baba spoke bitterly. " 'A man of means,' Mangal says. 'A man with his own shop.' A fairy tale my brother tells me to hurry us on our way." He stared hard at the man behind the gate. "How mean Uncle Jogu looks. He'll do no more for us than he feels he must."

It was true. Uncle Jogu was an irascible, miserly looking old man. Even Mangal had not claimed any good traits for him.

"Well, we are here and we will see what he has to say." *Baba* approached the stall.

Uncle Jogu approached. "Something for you?" he inquired. "Maybe a bangle for the young girl. Or a length of material. The woman could use a new *sari.*"

"We greet you, Uncle Jogu," *Baba* said, his hands folded in a *namaste.*

The older man's fawning manner changed to one of suspicion. "Who are you that you call me Uncle?" he asked.

"I am your sister Shalini's son," *Baba* answered.

"How do I know you are her son?"

"Ask me questions. Ask me who your father was, when he died. Ask me anything," *Baba* told him.

There followed a long recital of family members,

Baba supplying dates of death as further proof.

"You are who you say you are," Uncle Jogu acknowledged. "I suppose all of these are your family. You can see there is no room for you here while I do business and the stall is my only home."

"We have come a long way," *Baba* said.

"You have waited a long while to look me up and want help now, I warrant, or you wouldn't be here. I guess you can wait a few hours longer. I close my shop when darkness falls. You can come back then."

"We thank you," *Baba* said.

They trudged a short way down the street and then sat down on the walk as they saw others do. Meenu clung tightly to Mama as though in fear. Vashti thought the city was a wretched place. She hated being close to so many people and she felt sick from the odor of the gutter. Only Govind took a lively interest in the scene about him. He watched the beggars in the street and he was much impressed with the success of one bright-looking boy. A constant flow of *rupees* and *paise* (small coins) went into his pocket.

At dusk, the five of them arose.

"His place is so small. How can all of us get in there?" Mama asked.

Uncle Jogu opened the gate to receive them and then dropped and fastened the bamboo curtain closing the stall for the night.

"The woman will cook rice for us," he said.

He handed Mama an amount that was pitifully little for six people. She took it and set about her task.

Vashti played with Meenu keeping her awake so the child could claim her share of food.

As the days passed, the Kripal Prakash family was

to learn firsthand what Mangal had said. Uncle Jogu was not an easy person to live with. While they were with him *Baba* tried to find work. He walked miles each day going from factory to factory but the answer was always the same. No one had any use for a man without skills.

One night he came home enraged. He received his small ration of rice and stared at it with contempt. "It is all I can expect from my uncle when others regard me as an untouchable," he said.

"What do you mean?" Uncle Jogu asked. "We are of the Vaisya caste."

"Today I went to a dairy and asked for work. Milking cows is a lowly job but I was willing to do it. Do you know what they told me? Milk must be kept sanitary so they use an electric contrivance strapped to the animal to draw the milk from its udder. They were saying my hands were too unclean to touch the cows' teats. Then they had the gall to offer me a job cleaning the stalls!"

"It would have been a job," Uncle Jogu said.

"It is work for an untouchable," Mama defended her husband.

"Must I go on supporting his family? But if he is too good to work, maybe you can get a job."

"I don't know how to look," Mama murmured.

"I can direct you. I talked to a customer today who is leaving her mistress. If you go there tomorrow, you might take her place."

"I will go," Mama said.

"And you," he said, turning to *Baba*. "I will send you to a man who has a city job. Maybe he knows someone who will hire you."

When Mama came home next evening, she had employment.

"What do you do?" *Baba* asked.

"I am a sweeper," she answered.

The Hindu religion allocated such work to the untouchables but *Baba* made no outcry. It was not important that Mama should do the work of the *outcastes* since she was only a woman.

It was quite another story when *Baba* came in next evening. He had kept the appointment Uncle Jogu arranged through the man with a city job. He was so angry upon his return that he forgot he was dependent upon the older man for the food he and his family ate.

"You knew this man was a streetcleaner. You knew you were sending me to the city sanitation department!" he yelled.

"Yes, I knew," Uncle Jogu retorted. "Did you get the job?"

"Get the job? Have I fallen so low I must sweep up human waste from the gutter? Who am I that I should do such foul tasks?"

"Who are you?" Uncle Jogu roared. "You are a man who has turned down two jobs in a week. You are a man who will let his aged uncle feed you and your family when you could feed them yourself. Listen to me now. Tomorrow morning, out you go, all of you. And don't come back in the evening."

Baba looked at him in consternation. "You want us to live on the street?" he asked.

"Others do. Besides, that is your concern, not mine." Uncle Jogu remained hard as stone.

The next morning when all of them left the stall, Mama, carrying Meenu, went her way to her work.

Govind and Vashti followed their father in another direction.

Govind said, "I have money, *Baba.* See." He brought a few coins from his pocket.

"Paise and a few *rupees*!" his father exclaimed. "Where did you get them?"

"Begging," Govind answered.

"Begging!" *Baba* raised his voice in anger but Govind brought out more coins and still more coins. He placed all of them in his father's hands.

Baba looked at Vashti. "You could bring in a little money, too," he said.

Their life pattern was set. *Baba* rented a shanty in the *bustee,* no worse than some and better than others. Mama worked as a sweeper, Govind begged and Vashti, too, although she was never as successful at it as her brother was. *Baba* sat inside their one-room hut nursing his grudge against a society that could not offer a decent man of the Vaisya caste any work but that of the untouchables.

Vashti's thoughts had wandered so far from the milk shed that she didn't even notice when Mrs. Ghose left. She finished her milking chore, then balancing the milk vessel on her head, she joined the older lady. This must have been the evening when Mrs. Ghose's mind would not rest until she knew all of Vashti's story.

"With all the girls there are in Calcutta, how did it happen to be you who found your way here?"

"It was Miss Narain. She saw me once when we lived in the village when she was Govind's teacher. She told me about the Christian Brotherhood of Sharing. She works for them now," Vashti said.

"I know," Mrs. Ghose replied.

"The first time she saw me, Miss Narain promised she would try to get me into a school. Then we left the village and I thought I would never see her again. But she went back to Bajribasha and the neighbors told her we had gone to Uncle Mangal's in Bartoor. When she began working for the Christian Brotherhood she went to Uncle Mangal's. He sent her to Great-Uncle Jogu's who sent her on to our place in the *bustee*. Miss Narain is wonderful," Vashti said with fervor.

"She is a fine Christian lady," Mrs. Ghose said.

Vashti looked at her interestedly. "Are you a Christian?"

"I have been a follower of the Master for many, many years," Mrs. Ghose answered.

FAITH REFORMED LIBRARY
ROUTE 3 — BOX 19
KANKAKEE, ILLINOIS 60901

7

Good for Evil

Although she had not been lonely during October vacation, Vashti was glad to see her friends when school resumed. Until she saw Radha, she hadn't realized how much she had missed her. She had never had a close girl chum before, not even when she had lived in the village. And now she had other friends besides Radha. She was especially fond of Lata and Shoba and Shantha. She wondered if she and Purnima would ever be friends. They surely weren't now. Even though sixth grade mats went along well enough after the bad grade on her paper, Vashti couldn't feel very forgiving toward the one who had done her so much harm at exam time. And Purnima's dark eyes sent shafts of animosity in Vashti's direction every time their paths crossed.

Because the girls had all turned against her when there had been that trouble about the test paper, Purnima appeared to dislike Vashti more than ever. And the other students hadn't forgotten or forgiven Purnima when they returned to school in November. No on likes being shunned and Purnima was no exception.

"You'd think I was a leper the way they act," she muttered to herself.

She felt like retching when Vashti told the group in their hostel room that now she had been promoted to sixth grade in all her studies. Why should they be so pleased? The promotion didn't help them any.

Since she had no friends to talk to she decided she could at least please her parents by bringing home a good report card. They would probably give her some new *bangles* (bracelets) if she did. One way to do this, she thought, was to make the teachers like her. She began going from room to room after classes were over, asking if she could run any errands or help them in any way. Nor did she forget Miss Adhikari when she was trying to make a good impression. She frequented the principal's office and ran more errands for her than she did her classroom teachers.

One day Miss Adhikari sent her to the garden with a message for Mrs. Ghose. Purnima hoped Vashti wouldn't be working there. Even if she did think she hated her she had an uncomfortable feeling of guilt every time she passed the one she had deliberately hurt. Luck wasn't with her today because Vashti was in the garden. But Mrs. Ghose was nearer. She would deliver her message and not let on she knew Vashti was there.

Suddenly she froze where she stood. A cobra about six feet long poised facing her in the path. With its upper body standing erect about two feet from the ground, the snake expanded its hood until its dull gold head appeared flat. The cobra's lidless eyes stared at her banefully while its forked tongue flailed the air. In an instant, its head shot forward to sink its fangs into her leg.

Purnima found her voice and screamed in pain.

Mrs. Ghose rushed to the girl just in time to catch a glimpse of the snake as it glided off the path and disappeared among the pumpkin vines. It had discharged its poison; it would follow its normal way of life until it was disturbed again.

"My foot! I can't move it!" Purnima's shrill cry split the air.

Seeing the twin fang marks, Mrs. Ghose pulled the *palla*—the end of her sari—from her shoulder and tore a strip from it to use as a tourniquet.

"Vashti!" she called. But Vashti was there beside her and she saw the cobra's mark, too. "Go get the sharpest knife the cook has. Bring it to me as quick as you can."

Vashti darted away running faster than she had ever run before. She knew what Mrs. Ghose intended to do. She would cut through the flesh where the fangs had gone in and draw out the poisoned blood. Every second counted if Purnima were to live.

When she returned with the knife, Purnima was lying down on the garden path. Her face was drawn with agony. Her pitiful moans filled the air.

"Pray for her," Mrs. Ghose told Vashti as she took the knife.

How Vashti wished she could pray but, unlike the Christians, she could only make her entreaties before an image of her gods. She watched fascinated as Mrs. Ghose squatted beside Purnima and sank the knife carefully into the flesh of the girl's leg. She had to cut deep enough through the fang mark to dispel the venom, yet avoid cutting a vein. When she had made an incision about an inch long, she repeated the cut through the twin mark of the other fang.

Vashti knew what she must do. She could not bear to let Mrs. Ghose suck the venom from the wound into her own mouth. When the older woman laid the knife aside, Vashti gave her a push backward, upsetting her from her squatting position. Instantly, Vashti was on her knees, her mouth drawing the blood from Purnima's cut flesh.

Mrs. Ghose, trying clumsily to rise from where she lay on her back, shouted, "Spit it out! Spit it out!"

Vashti released the foul-tasting fluid from her mouth but immediately put her lips back to the open cuts to again draw out the poison. By the time Mrs. Ghose was on her feet again, the girl had filled her mouth and expelled the blood three times. The older woman forcibly moved her from Purnima by picking her up and setting her to one side. In a position to do what she had intended to do in the first place, Mrs. Ghose drew the blood and released it several times before she rose to her feet.

So intent had the woman and girl been that they hadn't been aware that a crowd had gathered. There were students, teachers and even the principal.

Miss Dal went to Purnima. She saw the girl's forehead beaded with the sweat of pain. Leaning over, she dried the perspiration with the corner of her *palla*.

"What kind of snake was it?" Miss Adhikari asked.

"Cobra," Mrs. Ghose told her briefly.

The principal dispatched two girls to bring a stretcher from the office. "Call Doctor Singh while you're there," she said.

"How do you feel?" she asked Mrs. Ghose.

"I'm fine—but look after Vashti," she said. "She drew the first blood, the blood that was really filled with venom."

Vashti was sitting on the ground near Purnima. She looked pale and shaken.

"We should have a hospital here," Miss Adhikari said. "But we must do with what we have. I'll take the three of you to my apartment," she said.

Radha and Lata bent over Vashti. "What happened?" Lata asked.

Vashti felt too wretched to talk. Her face had lost its paleness and taken on a greenish tinge.

"I think I'm going to be sick," she said. And promptly was.

But the litter was here now and two of the teachers lifted Purnima on to it. She whimpered like an animal in pain. Now the procession started toward Miss Adhikari's apartment, the stretcher bearers and the victim in the lead, Vashti following with Lata and Radha giving her support, and Mrs. Ghose coming next flanked by Miss Dal, the mathematics teacher, and Miss Adhikari, although the gardener refused any help, declaring she was fine. Following was a retinue of girls drawn by morbid curiosity as well as concern.

Miss Adhikari had Purnima moved to her own bed and she set up cots in the same room for the other two.

In spite of Mrs. Ghose's insistence that she was all right, she appeared grateful to lie down when her bed was ready.

When the principal had cleared the room except for the three patients, Mrs. Ghose faced Vashti. "You did a Christian act even if it was a foolish one when you took it upon yourself to draw out the poison."

"I didn't want anything to happen to you," the girl answered.

"I know, little one," Mrs. Ghose said.

Vashti kept thinking about her friend's remark that she had done a Christian act. How could she do a Christian act when she was not a Christian? Where did Christianity begin? She had only done what she felt she must.

Vashti Gains a Friend

Dr. Singh went quickly to Purnima and raised her eyelids to look at her eyes. He felt her limbs, her body, and ordered her to move her neck. When she complied, he gave a satisfactory murmur.

He filled his hypodermic needle. As he pushed it into her flesh, he reassured her soothingly. "This vaccine will check the effects of any poisons left in your system," he said.

"Am I going to get well?" Purnima asked hopefully.

"You are, indeed," he answered.

"I'm really going to live?" she asked as if unable to believe it.

"Probably until you are an old lady. I see no reason

to think differently now."

"But my foot. I can't move it. Will I be able to walk?" she asked.

"Your foot and all of you will be as good as ever before many days. You have much to be thankful for, young lady. You would be in death's agony now if it were not for the prompt attention you received."

"I'm going to be all right," she said in wonder. "Vashti, Mrs. Ghose, did you hear that? You two saved my life."

"Thank God," Mrs. Ghose said.

"I'm glad you're going to get well, Purnima," Vashti answered from her heart.

When Dr. Singh had left the house, Miss Adhikari came into the bedroom. "I'm happy to get a good report on my three patients," she said.

Mrs. Ghose struggled to a sitting position. "Two patients. I'm not sick." Then lying down again, she said, "Just a little bit lazy."

"And perhaps the stomach doesn't feel too good. Isn't that so? Anyway, the doctor said you must not work for at least three days. He left some pills for all of you to take and he told me you should remain here tonight," Miss Adhikari said.

"Mama Ghose and my husband, what will they think when I don't come home?" Mrs. Ghose asked anxiously.

"Don't worry. I'll send a messenger to tell them.

Turning to Purnima, Miss Adhikari said, "Dr. Singh thinks it would be best for you to return home for awhile. Your mother can look after you there. We have no one here to nurse the sick."

"When will I go?" Purnima asked.

"As soon as he thinks you are well enough to travel. I'll send you there in a motorcar," she explained. "And now, do any of you feel up to eating a little or would you rather forget the evening meal?"

The mention of food was nauseating to them all.

By morning, everyone was feeling considerably better and Mrs. Ghose said she was going back to her weeding in the garden.

Mention of the garden reminded the two girls of the snake. Both of them shivered.

"You can't go into the garden, Mrs. Ghose. The snake is still there and it might bite you," Vashti said.

At that instant, all of them heard a loud rap at the front door. Then a man's voice, well-known to Mrs. Ghose, was speaking to Miss Adhikari.

"How is my wife?" Hari Ghose was saying.

Mrs. Ghose wrapped her *sari* around her hastily and left the bedroom.

"Don't worry, husband. I am in good health. Why are you here? Aren't you working today?" she asked.

"The factory can get along without me for a while. I wanted to make sure you were all right," he told her.

"And now you see that I am."

"Yes. And I want to keep you that way. I'm going to hunt that cobra and kill it before you go back to your work in the garden."

She looked quickly to see how his feet were clad. She saw he was wearing boots instead of sandals.

"You are a good man, Hari, but I will go with you to kill the snake," she said.

"You are not well. You must stay here," he said.

Mrs. Ghose appealed to Miss Adhikari. "He shouldn't go out there alone. If the cobra should strike

95

there would be no one to look after him."

"You're right. I'll go with him and watch until he has found the snake and destroyed it," the principal told her.

"I'm going to take you home when I've finished the business in the garden," Mr. Ghose told his wife.

As he and Miss Adhikari were about to leave, Mrs. Ghose said, "Wait a minute. Miss Adhikari, will you let me take Vashti to our home until she is well again? My husband's mother loves to nurse and fuss over people."

Miss Adhikari looked from her employee to Mr. Ghose. He nodded his head.

"You may take her if you're sure you want the responsibility. You need not do it to make things easier for me," she said.

"We want her," Mrs. Ghose assured her. And then, "The cobra went into the pumpkin vines," she said.

Returning to the bedroom, she spoke to her young helper. "Vashti, I hope you are well enough to get up and ride in a *jutka*. My husband and I are taking you home with us."

"Where is your husband?" Vashti asked.

"He went to the garden to kill Purnima's cobra."

"Don't call it *my* cobra. I didn't want anything to do with it when it was alive and I wouldn't want to see it again even if it were dead," Purnima declared.

"All right. We shall call it the cobra of the garden. Perhaps it is a direct descendant of that shameless serpent that lived in the Garden of Eden."

"What serpent are you talking about?" Vashti asked.

"It is a story. It is the story of the snake that brought sin to the world and caused the downfall of man."

Perhaps she wanted to take her mind from the dangerous task Mr. Ghose had set for himself. At any rate, she said, "I think there is just time to tell it before husband comes back."

Vashti listened while Mrs. Ghose told the chronicle of Adam and Eve as it is recorded in Genesis.

"Do you know a lot of stories?" Vashti asked.

"I know the Word of God. I read the Bible every evening," Mrs. Ghose answered.

The girl wasn't sure Mrs. Ghose had answered her question but she supposed the Christians read the Bible just like Hindus read the *Ramayana*. Vashti remembered how, when she was very small, she had listened to the exciting stories about Rama and Sita and Ravana. The head man of the *penchayat* read to them from the *Ramayana* on festival days. When he died, none of the other village elders could read. The new head man recounted them as he remembered them, but they were not at all like the stories in the book. Even at that time Vashti wanted an education so that she could read the beautiful stories.

"It seems to me husband should be back by now," Mrs. Ghose said nervously.

"Don't worry. He'll kill the snake before it can harm him," Purnima said.

"Mrs. Ghose," Vashti said. "The cobra is a holy snake. Aren't you afraid evil will come to us if it is killed?"

Mrs. Ghose laughed. "One evil that will never touch us is the fangs of that cobra. Dead snakes don't bite. Vashti, God would never put a snake's life before a person's. He gave us dominion over all creatures."

Just then Mr. Ghose and Miss Adhikari returned to

97

the house. Mrs. Ghose sighed with relief.

"Did you find the cobra?" she asked.

"Found it, killed it and buried it," her husband answered.

"And I am forever in your debt," Miss Adhikari told him. "Since this happened yesterday, my girls have been afraid to step outside."

Before Vashti left, Purnima said to her, "I'm so ashamed for what I did to your test paper. I thought I hated you and I'm ashamed of that, too."

"You have no more reason to be ashamed than I have. I was not forgiving," Vashti admitted.

"But you had reason to be mad at me and I have no excuse for doing what I did to you," Purnima said.

Vashti reached across the bed and took her hand. "It's over and done with. We'll forget all about it."

Mr. Ghose did not look at all like Vashti expected him to look. Instead of being black-skinned like his wife, he was a light tan. He was not as tall as Mrs. Ghose but he was stockily built with big hands and feet.

Her second surprise was the size of the home in which they lived. When Vashti's father had his farm, the wealthiest man in the village had only a two-room house. The Ghose's home had four rooms—two for sleeping, one room where the family spent most of their time and a lean-to that had been added as a kitchen.

Mr. Ghose's mother was doll-size compared to his wife. She was roly-poly and she had an open smile and a lovable way of bossing people about.

She took command as soon as the two convalescents arrived and her son left to finish the day at the factory.

"So this is Vashti! My son's wife tells us about you every evening," Mama Ghose explained. She led her to one of the bedrooms. "You shall lie on my cot while I make up your bed in the living room."

"I really don't need to lie down," Vashti said.

"Yes, you must." Then turning to her daughter-in-law, she said, "Mutu, you lie down, too."

Mrs. Ghose grinned. "I am Mutu," she explained to Vashti.

Mama Ghose soon had Vashti's bed made up. She had padded it so well that the sick girl couldn't feel the cords lacing the cot from side to side.

"You are comfortable?" she asked her patient.

"Yes, thank you," Vashti answered.

"Would you like some lime juice and water?"

"I don't want to trouble you," the girl answered. She had never tasted lime juice. She wasn't sure she would like it.

"Go ahead. Fix it for her. It is good for her stomach," Mrs. Ghose called from the bedroom.

"Good for your stomach, too. I'll bring it to both of you," Mama answered.

After a little, she carried in the drinks from the kitchen.

"It is too bad you must be away from us in the bedroom," she said to her daughter-in-law. "When Hari comes home, I'll have him carry your bed into the living room."

"When Hari comes home, he will sit down and eat a supper I have cooked for him myself. It is nonsense that I should lie in bed when I am well enough to be up," Mrs. Ghose said.

"Stick out your tongue," Mama said and Mrs.

Ghose did as she was told. "You look well to me but we'll follow the doctor's orders until this afternoon. Then you shall get up and fix your rice *pilau* (rice boiled with fish). Mine never tastes as good as yours."

When Hari Ghose came home from work that evening he greeted Vashti as one of the family.

"It is good to have a young person in the house again," he said to his wife.

"Yes. Losing our girls to their husbands was like losing springtime. My little helper brings it back to us," Mrs. Ghose answered.

Vashti tasted the rice *pilau* but she ate very little of anything. She was still uncomfortable with cramps. Knowing their cause made food seem more unpalatable than it might have otherwise.

After supper, Mrs. Ghose took down the Bible and opened it to the book of Luke. She read about Jesus going to the home of a Pharisee to eat and how a woman who had been a great sinner came in. Being sorry for the life she had lived, she knelt at Jesus' feet and washed them with her tears and wiped them with her hair, then kissed them and rubbed them with costly ointment from an alabaster flask she carried.

His host thought Jesus should not permit a woman of bad character in His presence. Knowing what the Pharisee was thinking, Jesus said, "Simon, I have something to say to you. A certain creditor had two debtors; one owed 500 *denarii* (silver coins of Bible times) and the other owed 50. When they could not pay he forgave them both. Now which of them will love him the most?"

Simon answered, "The one, I suppose, to whom he forgave the most."

Jesus told him he had judged rightly and then He said, "I entered your house, you gave Me no water for My feet, but she has wet My feet with her tears and wiped them with her hair. You did not anoint My head with oil, but she anointed My feet with ointment. I tell you, her sins are forgiven for she loved much; but he who is forgiven little loves little." And He said to the woman, "Your sins are forgiven."

When Mrs. Ghose had finished her story she closed the Bible and put it back on the shelf. "Now, I am going to bed. I may not be as fit as I thought I was," she said.

Her husband looked alarmed. "Do you have pain? Maybe I should have the doctor look at you again."

"Don't bother, I'll be all right tomorrow," she answered.

"You must stay home though. You must take care of yourself," he admonished her.

When all of them had retired, Vashti lay on her cot and thought about the Bible story she had listened to. Besides being a man of love and compassion, Jesus was a man of justice. Radha said God had sent His Son to earth to teach us how to live so that we could be with Him in Heaven. The story tonight showed that God wanted us to treat other people fairly. She couldn't feel that the moneylender who took her family's home in the village had treated them fairly. He hadn't sought forgiveness either but Vashti felt she must forgive him for her own sake. She had held hate in her heart too long. It had become a rancid sore.

Next morning, when Mama Ghose had gone out to shop for the day's vegetables, Vashti said to Mrs. Ghose, "You have a nice house."

"My husband is a good provider. He is an overseer at

101

the linen factory," she answered.

"Oh," Vashti said. She wondered why Mrs. Ghose worked if she had no need to.

Mrs. Ghose understood. "The money is not needed in our home but I work at the school so that Mama can run the house and feel needed. I think it is sad to see old people sit and have nothing to occupy their time. Mama is a strong and healthy woman and she likes to be in charge here."

"I think you like to work, too," Vashti said.

Mrs. Ghose smiled. "I think you are right. And there are places to use the money. We help our church here. One of our daughters married a minister and we help his church, too. Our other son-in-law is a doctor in a mission hospital where there is always need. The patients who come to the clinic are too poor to pay."

Vashti thought Mrs. Ghose was a puzzle. She worked hard and then gave her money away. What would the world be like if everyone did that? she wondered—but it was foolish to think that way. There would never be a world of people like Mrs. Ghose.

"Have you always lived in Lorabad?" Vashti asked.

"I was born here but my father's people came from the south. As far back as anyone remembers they were fishermen there. My grandfather was different. He was not content to live on the beach and follow the occupation of his ancestors. With his young wife and their son he started moving inland. He went from place to place until he came to Lorabad. Here he found a community of men who spoke Telegu, his native tongue, and he stayed here. So my father really grew up in Lorabad even though he was born where our people live in the south."

"Do you speak Telegu?" Vashti asked.

"Very little. My father learned Hindi in school and the only time we spoke Telegu in our home was when Grandfather was there."

"Didn't your grandfather ever want to go back to his fishing village?" Vashti asked.

"He went back once but only to arrange a marriage for my father. He liked living inland," Mrs. Ghose answered.

"Is your husband from the village of your people?"

Mrs. Ghose laughed. "No. He was born here. I broke the family tradition. My daughters are the first who are not pure Dravidians. They have a lighter skin than I."

Vashti's big eyes opened wider. "Is that what a Dravidian is?" she asked.

"You didn't know? The Dravidians are one of the oldest races in India. We were here before the Aryans came. We are dark-skinned and many of us live from the fish of the sea."

The girl looked so confused that Mrs. Ghose became curious. "What did you think a Dravidian was?" she asked.

Vashti was very embarrassed. "I didn't know. When Miss Adhikari told me you were a Dravidian I thought, well I thought a lot of things," she finished lamely.

Mrs. Ghose began to chuckle. "And what were some of those thoughts that make you squirm when you think about them now?"

Vashti felt her face go hot. "I thought a Dravidian might be someone with sorcery powers," she admitted.

Mrs. Ghose's chuckle grew until it became a guffaw. Her whole body shook with enjoyment. Tears streamed down her face from her laughter.

"You thought I was a witch," she gasped. At last, bringing her outburst down to a chuckle again, she said, "Well, I guess I'm big enough to house a spirit if there were such things."

Still embarrassed, Vashti said, "When I knew you, I knew your power was for good and not evil."

Mrs. Ghose became serious. "Thank you, child. I hope I have that power for good; but if I have, it comes through the Lord Jesus Christ and not through witchcraft."

Mrs. Ghose went back to work at the school next day and came home carrying her young friend's schoolbooks.

"Miss Adhikari wants you to stay home the rest of the week. She thought you would want to study now that you feel better," she said.

Vashti was glad to have her books but most of all she looked forward to the evening hour when Mrs. Ghose read from the Bible. She learned that there was poetry as well as stories in the Book. The Psalms were beautiful and they praised God for all His wonders.

At the end of a week she was glad to return to school but she knew she would miss listening to Mrs. Ghose reading from the Bible each evening. Still, there was chapel, and Miss Adhikari told many interesting things about the Master.

9

The Welcoming

The girls in the hostel made Vashti feel she was a real heroine when she returned to school. They placed a garland of jasmine on her head. They welcomed her with posters that read, "Welcome, Vashti! We are proud of you."

Vashti had never been the center of attention before. Now she was embarrassed and felt she didn't merit such a show of esteem.

But Radha thought differently. "We should have arranged a parade and fireworks for you and we would have if we could have managed it."

"I never dreamed anything like this would ever happen to me." Vashti put up her hand and touched the wreath on her head as if not quite sure it was happening now. "But I don't deserve it and I don't know how to say 'thank you'."

"You do deserve it and you just now said it. I mean you said 'thank you.' So I guess that takes care of that. Now, let's get on with the celebration," Lata said.

Shantha uncovered a tray of *jelebies* and other sweets and Shoba opened several bottles of strawberry soda pop.

Vashti thought it was too much. Having a party was so exciting she was afraid she was going to be sick again. But after two *jelebies* and a swallow of pop, she settled down to enjoy herself.

"Now, tell us what happened," one girl said.

"You'll have to wait till Purnima comes back to school to hear the whole story. All I saw was that awful snake slithering off through the garden and the marks on Purnima's leg. She was crying and in no time at all she couldn't move that foot. She thought she was going to die."

"We were afraid she would die, too. And we were sorry we had treated her the way we did. It wasn't very Christian-like. We should have been more forgiving," Radha said.

"I think Purnima will always be my friend now," Vashti told them.

"Well, I hope so. You saved her life," Shoba replied.

"Not really. Mrs. Ghose was going to draw out the venom and I did what I did to keep her from doing it," Vashti explained.

"Hail to our modest heroine," Shantha cried.

And the girls all answered, "Hail."

Vashti glowed red, but more with pleasure than

with embarrassment. Yet she insisted, "I'm not a heroine."

"We think you are and you are an example to all of us," Lata said.

When lights were out and Vashti lay upon her cot, she pondered Lata's statement. Except for Shoba, all of these girls were Christian. How could she be an example in living for the followers of Christ? Looking at it from the other point of view, was she putting down the Hindu religion when she thought one of that faith could not be an example for Christians? It was all very confusing and before she had sorted out an answer she was asleep.

After Purnima had been home three weeks she returned to school. She wore a new blouse and several brightly colored bangles on her arm. When she and Vashti were alone, she said, "Hold out your hand."

Vashti did as she was told and Purnima slipped the bracelets from her arm onto Vashti's.

"No. You must not give me your pretty bangles," Vashti protested.

"I must because it's what I want to do," she said. "If I had mentioned it, my father would have bought some trinkets for you, too. But it seemed more like giving if I gave something of my own."

Vashti's eyes filled with tears. She no longer cared whether or not the girls knew about her poverty background. "I live in Calcutta's *bustee* where everything is ugly and even the air smells foul. These are the first pretty things I've ever owned. Thank you."

"You don't need to thank me. I feel so good because you would let me give them to you," Purnima said. Now she spoke rather shyly. "The minister of our church called a meeting of thanksgiving because I was alive after being bitten by a cobra. He prayed for you, too, Vashti."

"He did? What did he say?" Vashti asked.

"He prayed that you would have a long life so that you could go on doing acts of goodness for other people," Purnima told her.

Vashti showed great interest. "Did he say my name?" she asked.

"Vashti Prakash, that's what he said," her friend told her.

"Imagine that," Vashti thought to herself. "A minister of the Christian religion had spoken to his God and asked these things for me, Vashti Prakash."

"There is just one thing I want to ask of you," Purnima said. "Miss Adhikari told me to take my books with me when I went home to study so I wouldn't get behind in my classes. I think I'm up on everything but mats. It's my poorest subject and I wonder if you will help me?"

The request had cost Purnima a great sacrifice of pride and Vashti knew it. "I'll be glad to do what I can," she answered.

The days went by swiftly and pleasantly. The girls in Vashti's hostel room found living together much more comfortable since they no longer kept Purnima outside their circle. Actually, it was no effort to include her in everything they did. She had become a different person since being bitten by the cobra in the garden. As Lata put it, "I think Vashti sucked out more than snake venom from Purnima's leg. She drew out the meanness, too."

As November days slid by and December was

almost upon them, the girls began talking about December vacation days. To Shoba, it merely meant seeing her family again. To Vashti, it meant less than that. She had no means of getting to Calcutta. But to most of the girls, the Christian girls, it meant the celebration of Christmas.

"What is Christmas like?" Vashti asked Radha one day when they were alone.

"It's the day we observe Christ's birthday," Radha said.

"Do you mean Jesus who was the Son of the Christian God?"

"Yes. At Christmas everyone thinks of the Baby and how great God was to lend Him to the people on the earth for a time. But the festivities are not the same everywhere."

"How is it in your home?" Vashti asked.

"Our celebration is so bound up with the church since *Baba* is minister that I'd have to tell you about what we do at home and church both," Radha answered.

"Go on. What do you do at home and church?" Vashti urged her.

"Well, back home they will already be getting ready for December 25. The children's choir leader will be teaching them Christmas carols. Mama has probably opened up the annual mission box of clothing and is trying to decide who is in more dire need because most of them would welcome something new to wear. And the whole membership is thinking about the musical play we put on every year."

"What is it like?" Vashti asked.

"It opens with someone singing a woeful song about

all the troubles that are in the world. Then the whole church goes dark and there is a noise like a great clap of thunder, and lightning shoots across the sky. (It's really a moving spotlight that is blackened except for a tiny spot.) When everything is dark again, you hear God's voice through the angel Gabriel. It is so loud it almost shakes the church. He speaks to Mary and He tells her she is going to bear God's Son. When the voice dies away, the curtain comes back and there is Mary and her cousin, Elizabeth. They are clutching each other and they are full of fear and yet they are full of joy because this wonderful thing is going to happen to Mary. They sing a song of praise to God, but Mary wonders why she, a person of lowly stature, was chosen to bear God's Son."

"And what happens next?" Vashti asked.

"The chorus sings how Mary and Joseph, her betrothed, must go to Bethlehem to register their names. Mary is almost ready to give birth to God's Son. You see Joseph knocking on a row of doors trying to find a place for Mary to stay, but the rooms at all the inns are taken. Finally, one person says she can sleep in the stable."

"Was Jesus born that night?" Vashti asked.

"Yes. When the curtain opens again, you see the inside of the stable. The Baby is already born. Mary is holding Him, and Joseph hovers over both of them. Gathered around the holy family are the animals: cows, donkeys, sheep and doves."

"Real animals?" Vashti asked.

"Not real. They are made of heavy cardboard and propped up so they can stand. But the light in the stable shines on Mary and the Child. It's sort of dark where the animals are so they look real. Now we have people who sing and each one is supposed to be the voice of an animal. Each animal tells how honored he feels to share his stable with God's Son. After that, the humble shepherds come and worship and, last of all, the Wise Men come from the East. They pay homage to the Baby and give costly gifts. That is the end of the play."

"Is all of it sung?" Vashti wanted to know.

"There are places where words are spoken because they show more reverence that way. But most of the play is sung," Radha said.

"It sounds beautiful. What is Christmas like in your home?"

"The musical play is on Christmas Eve. At home, we get up on Christmas morning and *Baba* always reads the Christmas story from the Bible."

"Do you think Miss Adhikari will read the Christmas story in chapel before the school closes for vacation?" Vashti asked.

"Of course she will! When *Baba* has finished reading the story we have prayers and then breakfast. After breakfast, we give presents to one another, not big things but something we've made that shows our love. Mama fixes a special Christmas dinner and we have the old and unwanted people of the church at our table to make sure they have a good meal on festival day. In the afternoon, the children come to our door and sing the Christmas songs they have been practicing. *Baba* asks them in and Mama gives them *papaw* (papaya) and other snacks. Then they go on to other homes."

"Is that all?"

"Yes. After the work we have put in on the church program and the excitement of Christmas at home, we are about ready to collapse. We usually go to bed early," Radha told her friend.

"It sounds like a wonderful time. I can see why all of you Christians look forward to it," Vashti exclaimed.

Vashti was to have her vacation, too. Before school closed down, Miss Adhikari called her into the office.

"I've heard from Miss Narain," she said. "She is coming here for you and she will take you to your home for the holidays."

The news made Vashti feel like singing. She would not have Christmas like Radha but she would be with her family for ten days.

10

Vashti's First Christmas

As December advanced, the hostel became a beehive of activity. Except for Vashti and Shoba, all the girls in the room had Christmas gifts underway.

Being of the Hindu religion, Vashti had no reason to make gifts for the Christmas festival. But as she watched the girls stitching *cholis* (short-sleeved blouses worn with *saris*) and *angochas* (scarves), as well as children's toys, she wished that she could make a gift as a surprise for Mama and Meenu. She had a needle and thread (Miss Narain had included them among her things when she prepared her for school) but she had no material to use.

Seeing her interest, Shantha give her some bright

purple scraps that were left after she had cut a *choli* for her sister-in-law. Lata showed her how to cut the small pieces to make a doll. She added a scrap of fawn brown for Vashti to use for the face.

Until now, Vashti's sewing had been limited to mending her own clothes. She was awkward at putting the doll together, but her sewing was a labor of love and she stuck with it until it was finished. She stitched the eyes and nose and mouth on the doll's face and she had to admit it had turned out very well. How pleased Meenu would be to have a toy to play with! She could take it with her when Mama went out as a sweeper and keep herself entertained while Mama worked.

If only she had something to take to her mother!

It was almost as if Radha read her mind but she spoke regretfully. "I have this skirt I have outgrown. I wish I could give it to you so you could make it over into a garment for your mother or sister. But I promised I would bring it home so Mama could give it to one of the poor in our church."

Presently, Purnima sauntered over carrying a skirt of a lovely cerise shade.

"Vashti, could you use this thing for any of your sewing? It's no good to me. It's torn." She held it up to show a big hole near the hem.

"Purnima, it is so pretty. Let me mend it and you can wear it again," Vashti said.

"Such a long tear would look bad no matter how well you mend it," Purnima said. "Besides, I'm getting a new skirt for Christmas and I don't need this one."

"If you aren't going to do anything with it yourself, I could make a *choli* for Mama. She would look so

114

pretty wearing that color," Vashti said wistfully.

"Then it's yours," Purnima said and dropped it in Vashti's lap.

Radha helped Vashti cut the blouse and, by cutting carefully, there was enough left over to make an *angocha,* too.

That evening, as they walked to the milk shed, Shoba said, "You didn't know it but Purnima tore that skirt on purpose so she could give it to you."

"Are you sure?" Vashti asked.

"Yes. I saw her do it."

Vashti felt a warm rush of affection for the girl who had once been her enemy. "I wish she hadn't torn it." She walked on, quietly thoughtful. As she and Shoba parted to go each to her own buffalo, Vashti said, "I don't think I could have done it."

"Done what?" Shoba asked.

"I don't think I could have spoiled such a pretty skirt just so I could give it away."

"She wouldn't have done it for any of the rest of us. I guess she wants to make amends to you," Shoba answered.

"It's silly because she has no reason to make amends. I've quit thinking about that examination grade. I wish she would," Vashti answered. "But Mama will love the *choli.* I can just see her when I give it to her. She has never had anything so pretty. Purnima's clothes are all nice."

"Yes and her family really can't afford to spend all that money on her. I think they've treated her like a little princess and that's why she grew up acting like she did."

"She's changed now," Vashti reminded her.

School was dismissed on December 23. After classes, Vashti was getting the things together that she would need when she went home.

What would she take of her own personal belongings? True, she hadn't much—just the few extras that were in the package Miss Narain had left with her. She would not need her bowl that she carried when she went to her meals and she would not take any books or paper or pencils. She felt they were property of the school and shouldn't be carried away.

In the end, she took a gown to sleep in and a few *neem* twigs so she could keep her teeth clean. Nothing more. She wasn't sure why she was reluctant to take any clothing except the skirt and blouse she wore. Maybe it was because she didn't want to flaunt her good fortune before her poorly dressed family. Or maybe it was because she felt that everything that went into the *bustee* became contaminated. Or maybe neither of these reasons was the true reason.

Now that the day had actually come when she was leaving school to see her family, she had mixed emotions. The thought of going into the foul streets of Calcutta was repugnant but it would be so good to see Mama and Meenu again. And *Baba* and Govind, too, she added mentally, feeling guilty that she had omitted them in her first thoughts of home.

She recalled that first night here at school and how lonely she had been. She had changed a lot since then. And she'd accomplished a lot, too. She had overcome her homesickness, she had passed through fifth grade into sixth, she had made good friends, some like Mrs. Ghose whom she loved almost as much as if they were family. And all this had happened in a few months.

116

She loved school. She loved everything about it. Should she let her father know that she had not gone to the temple last Sunday to worship Mitra so that she might go with Radha to the chapel where Miss Adhikari told the story of Christ's birth and the girls sang carols? She had told herself it was only the singing she wanted to hear but she knew she wanted to hear how the Baby was born in a lowly stable and how the shepherds from nearby and the Wise Men from far off had come to worship Him there. She decided this was one of the things she could not mention at home. *Baba* might think she had thoughts of becoming a Christian. Of course, she hadn't such thoughts, but what if he should think so and force her to leave the school?

One of the pleasantest things about the trip home was seeing Miss Narain again. Vashti thought both Miss Narain and Miss Adhikari must be of Brahman caste. They were alike in many ways. The two were educated and both had features and coloring that spoke of high birth. But they differed in some respects. Miss Adhikari was very efficient. She had been kind to Vashti and so considerate that the girl felt she owed her a great deal. But she did not have the warmth that drew people to her. Miss Narain had this warmth. Perhaps it was necessary for a principal to be as Miss Adhikari was in order to keep a school running properly. But Vashti knew the trip to Calcutta was going to be much more enjoyable riding with Miss Narain than it would be if she were sitting beside Miss Adhikari.

Now when someone called to her that her ride had arrived, Vashti looked around the hostel room. The other girls had left earlier so she had no one to bid farewell. She turned to Radha's picture of Christ.

"Good-bye," she whispered, then picking up her small bundle she hurried down the stairs.

After their first greeting, Miss Narain looked her up and down with a smile.

"Well, where is that skinny child I brought here not many months ago? I see a nicely filled-out young schoolgirl," she said.

"I've had to let out the waistbands on both my skirts," Vashti confided.

"And that blouse is pulling tight, too. I hope you don't burst the seams while you are away," her companion said.

They got into the automobile and set off at a breathtaking speed. At least it seemed so to Vashti. After a little, she settled back in her seat. The cows, the fields of wheat and gram and barley, the villages were seen in a flash and were instantly replaced by other cattle, fields and villages.

Miss Narain glanced her way now and then, delighted at the girl's enjoyment. When she saw some of the novelty was wearing off, she said, "You are different."

"I feel different. I don't know why. Sometimes I feel like the things that happened to me before I went to school happened to another girl."

"You are becoming the person you were meant to be. I've kept pretty close tabs on you. I know you have the ability to soak in everything you read. I know, too, that you have a great capacity for living and loving. What do you want to do with your life?"

"You mean when I have gone through tenth grade at school? What can a person of my caste do?" she asked.

"Forget about going only as far as the tenth grade.

Forget about caste. What would you like to do more than anything in the world?" Miss Narain asked.

"Teach school," Vashti answered promptly.

"Then hold to that ambition," her older friend advised her. "Are you terribly excited about going home for a few days?"

There was the slightest hesitation. "I want to see my family," Vashti answered.

"But you can't bear the thought of going into the *bustee*," Miss Narain finished for her.

Vashti tried to explain her reluctance. "It is so nice at school. It's more than just a place to learn. The buildings and the courtyards are clean and neat. And the food! No wonder I'm getting fat. I've never had so much to eat."

"Some of the girls complain about the food," Miss Narain told her.

"How could they?" Vashti asked her, aghast.

"Perhaps they had more of a variety at home. But I agree with you. It is ample and well-cooked," her companion answered.

"No girls in our room complain," Vashti told her.

"That's good." And then her friend added, "I know how you must feel about going into the section of the city where your parents live. Someday perhaps you can move them out of there. Right now you will have to be careful. You are no longer a little waif who begs on the street."

Vashti colored at mention of her begging.

"Don't be embarrassed," Miss Narain admonished her. "What were you to do? One needs to exist. But as I was saying, you are not a pitiful-looking child now. You are a teenager who will soon be a lovely young lady. Girls who look like you aren't always safe on the street when they go out by themselves."

Vashti had only a glimmer of the meaning of such danger, but she knew girls and boys in the village were kept apart until their wedding nuptials.

"I don't suppose I'll ever marry," she said. How could she? she asked herself. There was no money for a wedding and she had no dowry. Her family hadn't a single thing worth giving, not even to the person who made the wedding arrangements for a husband. Besides, if life could go on as pleasantly as it was now, she didn't want to marry.

"You have a long while to consider whether or not you want a husband. You may change your mind," Miss Narain answered.

At last they were coming into Calcutta. It was dusk and lights came on as they entered the city.

Now Vashti saw homes set well back from the street. Some were two-story and all were plastered and painted white. Trees gave shade to the houses, curly-leafed asoka trees, date and coconut palms. Yellow jasmine and bright-colored dahlias gave the homes a happy look.

"Wouldn't it be nice if everyone lived such good lives that they were born the second time to riches such as these people have?" Vashti asked.

Miss Narain smiled at her sadly. "It would be nice if there was no poverty here, although pretty homes and riches don't always mean happy people. But you know we Christians don't believe we come back a second time to this earth."

Vashti looked interested. "If you don't come back in another life, where do you go?"

"We hope to live in a way that is pleasing to God while we are here and then go on to our heavenly home when this life is over," Miss Narain explained.

"What is it like—your heavenly home?"

"No one really knows. But Jesus said before He left this earth that He was leaving to prepare a place where we might all be with Him. He is God's Son so it must be a very splendid place," Miss Narain said.

Vashti thought for a few minutes about the Christian Heaven, wondering what it would be like. If it was splendid it must be very like the places they were passing now. Who could want more than a home such as these?

The traffic was heavier now and Miss Narain could not pass the bicycles and bullock carts and horse-drawn conveyances.

"Would you mind staying at my house tonight? If we go on, it will be quite late before we reach your part of the city," she said.

"I don't mind at all," Vashti answered. Indeed she felt a wave of relief followed by guilt. She shouldn't dread so much going into the *bustee*. If her people lived there day in and day out, she shouldn't shrink from visiting the place, she thought.

Later, as she luxuriated in the pink tub set into Miss Narain's pink and white bathroom, she wondered how it would feel to live like this all the time. Her hostess had given her a bar of flower-scented soap and told her to use anything she saw and liked on her hair and skin. It seemed very strange that one of the Brahman caste would invite a Vaisya into her home and share her own things with her. But Vashti happily applied oil to her hair after she had washed it.

She stood before the mirror, her hands mechanically plaiting her braids. Miss Narain said she would soon be a lovely young woman. She scrutinized the girl who looked back at her. Except for her filled-out face and the high gloss the oil had given her hair, she couldn't see much difference between the person she was now and the plain person she had always been. Probably Miss Narain had said what she said because she was a kind person and wanted Vashti to think well of herself. She wound her braids into a knot at the nape of her neck to see how she would look when she was older. The school had a rule that the girls could not put up their hair until they were 15. They must wear skirts, not *saris*, until they reached that age, too. Nevertheless, she was nearing adulthood and it would be well for her to start thinking seriously about life and the problems one met.

Tomorrow morning she would come face to face with the problems of a million lives, the slums of Calcutta.

When she and Miss Narain started out next day, her benefactress seemed especially gay.

"When I leave you, I'm going to my parents' home in the hills," she told Vashti. "We'll stop at the market and I'll get a few things to take with me."

The food center was an amazing place. Here were servants as well as matrons, their faces half-covered by their *saris' pallas*. They examined flowers and fruit and fish, spices and food grain. Vashti gazed about her, entranced by the exotic array, loving the mingling odors until they neared the meat section. The smell of the forbidden fresh beef was almost more than she could stand.

"My mother has no market like this where she can shop. I like to take her certain spices and fruits," Miss Narain explained.

She had brought two bags with her. "You carry one and I'll carry one and we'll fill them up as we go along," she said to Vashti.

Into each bag went pomelos, guavas, oranges, ginger root, tamarinds, peppers, and all the fruits and spices to make chutney. Rice was added to the bag Vashti carried. Last of all, passing through the fish market, Miss Narain bought two gleaming fish, their irridescent scales showing first pink, then green, then silver. She handed one to Vashti and carried the other herself.

She paused near the flower stand as they were leaving. "I'd like to buy flowers," she said. "But I don't see how we could possibly carry them." Regretfully, she walked on.

They stowed the bags of food in the automobile and drove away.

The streets they passed through became poorer and then, too soon, they came to the *bustee*. The foul stench reached them before they actually arrived.

Even riding in the automobile, Vashti began to feel closed in. People were everywhere. Young women, women who were probably young in year count but broken in health, hags, men, boys, girls, babies, most of them wearing filthy rags if they were covered at all. Children who might be as old as ten wandered without a piece of cloth to hide their bareness. Holy men chanted their way through the motley crowd, naked except for ashes, yellow paint and cow dung spread over parts of their bodies, the hair on their heads so

123

matted and tangled they resembled bramble bushes.

Miss Narain drove very slowly down the busy thoroughfare. It was impossible for her to do more than keep pace with the herd of people that milled the streets. Gaunt faces constantly appeared at the car window and wailed the beggar's cry, *"Baksheesh! Baksheesh!"* She had prepared herself for the siege with a collection of *paise* and even some *rupees* handily placed on the dashboard. Hollow-eyed women carrying stick-legged babies were the most frequent supplicants.

"They tell us the government is taking care of these people and we should ignore them. Look at them! Bundles of rags, or worse, no rags to hide their starving bodies. How can one pass by and not give to them?" she asked.

Vashti saw there were tears in her eyes.

Yet children had the natural desire to play. Some squatted over the drain building a dam. A few feet away another child squatted to defecate into the same water they played in.

All drivers were not as considerate as Miss Narain. Some plowed their way along, scattering the crowds with their horn blasts as they went. Such a driver knocked down a little one to avoid hitting a cow. The small boy was instantly on his feet and limped to the side of the street. Miss Narain stopped traffic to leave her car and go to him.

"Are you all right?" she asked.

"Yes, Miss," he replied.

Except for scraped skin, he showed no signs of injury. She gave him a few *paise* and went back to continue on her way.

She did not go far before she was forced to a stop. A cow so starved that its bones came through its hide staggered at snail's pace ahead of them. Finally, unable to go further, it lay down in the street directly in front of them.

Miss Narain looked dismayed. "I can't make that creature get up. I can't even ask someone else to do it," she said.

The traffic behind her was already pressuring her with horn blasts.

"The cow is getting ready to die," Vashti said.

"Yes," her older friend agreed. Little by little she inched her way around the animal and continued her slow progress down the street.

The retinue of beggars followed them.

"*Baksheesh! Baksheesh,* kind lady. No mother, no father, no family." This time the pitiful wail came from the lips of a young boy who had appeared at the car window.

"Govind!" Vashti cried.

"Vashti! Miss Narain!" Govind had the grace to blush.

"Hello, Govind," Miss Narain said pleasantly. She signaled and stopped, then opened the car door. "I'm glad you came along. I can't drive to your home for there is no street leading to it. When I let you out you can walk with Vashti there. She may not be safe on the street by herself."

Govind climbed in, taking in his sister's appearance from her head to her toes.

"You don't look the same," he said.

Now his gaze shifted to survey the mechanism of the car. He had never been inside one before.

11

Home to the Bustee

Miss Narain drove slowly down the crowded street, Vashti in the middle and Govind nearest the outer door.

The boy divided his interest between the car itself and the people on the street. He settled back trying to appear nonchalant, but his eyes gave him away. How he wished some of his friends could see him! At last he was rewarded.

"Narayan!" he called to a ragged boy who appeared to be a little older than himself.

Friend Narayan straightened from his humble begging posture before a tourist. "Govind!" he shouted. Not waiting for the few *paise* he had hoped to receive from the foreigner, he pushed his way into the traffic.

Loping alongside the automobile, he said, "What are you doing in that motorcar? Are you being taken to the courts?"

"No. Miss Narain asked me to get in and take a ride. She's a friend of mine," Govind bragged. "And this is my sister," he added, indicating Vashti.

"I was Govind's teacher," Miss Narain explained.

"Teacher?" Narayan appeared shocked. "You're not going to go to school, are you?" he asked Govind.

"Naw. My sister goes to school but I don't go for that old studying stuff," Govind declared.

Miss Narain's patience had reached the breaking point. "Look, Narayan, I can hardly maneuver through these streets under the best conditions and you're making it more difficult for me." She handed him a few coins. "Leave us now and continue this conversation with Govind at another time."

The street boy accepted the money and worked his way to a safer spot at the edge of the pavement.

"You'll be getting out soon," she said to the two young people in the seat beside her. "We must arrange a time and place to meet when I take you back to school," she said to Vashti.

"You met me at Uncle Jogu's stall before. I can wait for you there if that is all right with you," Vashti answered.

"Fine. I'll be there the morning of the New Year," she said. She worked her car to the edge of the thoroughfare. "This is the best place to let you out." she added, opening the door.

Vashti picked up the package she had brought from

the school. "Thanks for driving me home and for having me at your place last night."

"I've enjoyed every minute we were together," Miss Narain answered. To Govind, she said, "You look like a strong young man. There is a bag of things from the market in the back. Will you get it and carry it home?"

"Miss Narain!" Vashti said, surprised. "You didn't buy all those good things for us, did you? I thought you were taking them to your mother."

"The bag you carried is my Christmas gift to you and your family."

Govind lifted it out.

"You've done so much for me. I wish there was something I could do for you," Vashti said.

"Just have a nice vacation," Miss Narain said, closing the door and putting the car in gear.

"Merry Christmas!" Vashti called after her.

Miss Narain lifted her hand and waved as she worked her way into the traffic.

"She's pretty nice for an old school teacher," Govind said.

"She isn't a teacher now. She works for the Christian Brotherhood of Sharing," Vashti answered.

"What did you mean when you said Merry Christmas to her?" Govind asked.

"Christmas is the name of the day the Christians celebrate the birth of the Son of God," Vashti explained.

"You'd better not let *Baba* hear you say 'Merry Christmas.' Not if you want to go back to school," Govind warned her.

"I only said it because the Christian girls said it to one another when they were leaving. How is *Baba*?"

129

"You mean is he the same old *churail* (evil spirit) he was when you went away? He's just as mean."

"Govind! How do you dare to say such things?" Vashti demanded.

"I dare because he is a devil and you know it. But I'm not afraid of him," her brother declared.

As they talked they picked their way across the street. Govind walked with the assurance of one who is in his element. He forced a bicyclist and a man driving an oxen cart to come to a stop. Arriving on the other side, the boy and girl followed a path that led them beside a store building and, farther on, past a row of shanties.

Flies swarmed everywhere. The smell of garbage and animal and human waste was so strong Vashti could hardly keep from gagging. Yet she was on her way home and her heart beat faster knowing she would soon see Mama and Meenu. And *Baba,* of course.

"Shall I carry the bag for a ways now, Govind?" she asked. How good Miss Narain was to buy all those things for Vashti's family! The fruit and spices would be a real treat for everyone. And she wondered how long it had been since her people had tasted fish.

"I'll keep the bag until we get almost home. Then you can take it. You know how *Baba* is. He thinks women should carry anything like this. Not that I care what he thinks, but I don't want him to start off in a worse humor than his usual one," Govind said.

Vashti studied her brother. She thought he had changed more than she had. She wasn't sure it was all for the good. He acted like an adult instead of a boy of 11. He showed consideration for her but he was too knowledgeable, too self-assured in a swaggering sort of way. He looked healthy enough and she was grateful for this. Evidently, all his begging money didn't find its way home. He surely must be eating better than the rest of the family.

He interrupted her thoughts. "You carry it now," he said, handing her the bag of food.

And soon they came to their home, if such a structure could be called home. The Prakashes lived in one room of a row of houses. They were built of *kutka* (unbaked bricks) and the rains were gradually washing them away.

The brother and sister went inside. It was a little while before Vashti could adjust to the half-light. The room had only one small window.

"Well, Vashti, you come home," *Baba* greeted her. "Did the fine lady go back on her word or couldn't you learn?"

"Hello, *Baba*. I'm home for only a few days. School was dismissed for the Christmas festival," Vashti explained.

"Christmas? I never heard of that festival. We did not celebrate festivals of all the gods but I thought I knew the celebration days," her father said.

Vashti could see him plainly now. He squatted on the earthen floor, a petulant, disgruntled man. His once muscular body sagged in loose folds of skin. Her mention of the Christmas festival had been a mistake.

"It is not a day we celebrate. It is a Christian holiday," she told her father.

"So you are being taught about the Christian holidays! The woman who came here said you could remain of Hindu faith even if the school was Christian," her father said.

"I learned about Christmas only because I heard the girls talking," Vashti said.

"Shut your ears to such talk. You are a Hindu."

"Yes, *Baba*," Vashti answered.

"I see you are putting on weight. Those Christians have a motive in feeding you well. They believe a full stomach will win you over. I have permitted you to go to school to learn so you can earn many *rupees*, but you are to remain what you are—a Hindu."

"Yes, *Baba*," Vashti repeated. She wished Mama and Meenu would come home. She picked up the water jug. "I'm going to the water tap," she said.

Govind hadn't spoken since he came in. Now he said, "I'll go with you."

"Are you a girl child that you must go with your sister?" Mr. Prakash demanded.

"Then I won't go to the water tap. I'll go hunt up Narayan," Govind answered.

"You stay away from that boy. He is a good-for-nothing and he'll get you into trouble," *Baba* shouted as Govind walked out the door.

Vashti was sorry he was gone. She would be alone with *Baba* until Mama and Meenu came home. But she could keep herself busy. When she came back with water she would give the room a good cleaning.

She saw she must wade through mud where water had run from the faucet. The ways of the *bustee* were coming back to her. Not only those who lived here but people from the street used the tap for their morning ablutions, a ritual of the Hindu religion. Thank goodness, December was not the month of rains. During that season she had to wade in mud almost up to her knees to fill the water vessel.

"Shall I cook you a little rice gruel or make you a *loochi*?" she asked her father when she returned to the house.

"Do you think in your absence I have become a *sardar* (nobleman) so that I eat three times a day? You forget quickly that the Prakash family is in ill favor with the gods."

"I haven't forgotten and I know it is not your habit to eat at midday. But Miss Narain took me to the bazaar and she bought a bag of food such as we can never afford and sent it with me," Vashti explained.

"I'll eat no food that has been touched by a Christian," her father declared.

"Yes, *Baba*," Vashti answered.

"What is in the bag?" Mr. Prakash asked.

"Some pomelos, oranges, other fruits and spices. Things like that and a big fish and rice and wheat flour, too," she said.

"You can peel an orange for me," *Baba* said.

She did as he asked. The piquant smell made her mouth water and she ate the rind she removed. After her father had eaten the orange, he asked for another. She hoped there would be enough so that the others could have some, too.

She did what she could to clean the house and when it was time for Mama to come home she started a fire and heated water. She tried to listen for her mother's and Meenu's footsteps, but all sound was drowned out by an angry dispute going on in the next room. When her mother came through the door she was so glad to see her that she wanted to rush into her arms. Only family reticence held her back.

"Hello, Mama," she said shyly.

"Vashti! I didn't know you were coming."

Vashti read her homecoming welcome in her mother's eyes. "We have vacation days," she said. She went to Meenu and put her arms around her. "Hello, little sister. I've brought you a present."

Meenu had never learned to speak words but she smiled.

Vashti opened the package she had brought and took out the doll. She held it in her arms as if rocking it to sleep. "See. It's a baby. Meenu's baby," she said handing it to her little sister.

Meenu took it and examined it closely. Her fingers touched its eyes and nose and mouth. She imitated Vashti, rocking it back and forth, then she held it out to look at it again.

"I brought some things for you, too, Mama. They aren't new but they're nice." She handed her mother the *choli* and *angocha*.

Her mother gazed at them in wonder. "Oh, what beautiful material. How pretty the color," she said.

"I made them for you," Vashti said.

"What a nice job you did. Your stitches are so small," Mama answered.

"I hope the *choli* fits," Vashti said anxiously. Looking at her mama, she was afraid it might be too large. Mrs. Prakash was thinner than she had ever seen her, even in famine times.

"Where did you get the cloth?" her mother asked.

"One of the girls at school gave it to me. It had been a skirt but she tore it."

Now Mr. Prakash spoke up. "And what did you bring your *baba,* Vashti?" he asked.

"I'm sorry but I don't have anything for you, *Baba.*

You know I get no money at school. It was only through the girls' kindness that I could bring something to Mama and Meenu."

"Would it not have been better to give to your father than to give to your mother?" he demanded.

"But Mama goes to work every day. She has to go out on the street and I knew her *choli* was patched and worn," she said.

"Would I not be going to work every day, too, if the gods had treated me fairly? Or is it that you think I, a Vaisya, should clean streets? Your father should do the work of the untouchables. Is that what you want?" he asked, his voice rising.

Mrs. Prakash had begun coughing and Vashti knew the argument had upset her. She tried to smooth her father's injured feelings. "No, *Baba*. You should not do the work of the untouchables. And I am sorry I didn't bring you anything."

"You should be. Was I not a good father to you when I still had land? Did I not feed you and clothe you as long as I could?"

"Yes, *Baba,* you did and I promise to bring you a present next time I come home," she answered him.

Eager to have peace in the family, Mrs. Prakash said, "You hear, husband? You will have something fine, too. We have a good daughter."

"Mama," Vashti said, trying to divert *Baba's* attention. "The water is hot and we can have a very special meal tonight. Look at all these things Miss Narain sent to us."

Mrs. Prakash looked unbelievingly at the food Vashti had set out. "Fruit," she gasped. "And a fine fish! So many kinds of spices! More even than my em-

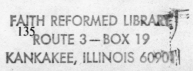
FAITH REFORMED LIBRARY
ROUTE 3 — BOX 19
KANKAKEE, ILLINOIS 60901

ployer has in her kitchen. We'll have the fish tonight with hot spices and rice. After supper, I'll make chutney. We'll eat well while you are here, Vashti."

"You will eat well," her husband remarked sourly. "I'll have none of the Christian's food."

"As you please, husband. If you eat none of it, there will be more for the rest of us," Mrs. Prakash answered.

Vashti was surprised at her mother's show of spunk. Was Mama no longer afraid of *Baba*, or did she no longer care what happened?

Meenu began to cough. It had a dry sound. Vashti was sitting on the floor and she pulled the child down into her lap. She felt Meenu's face. It was warm and the skin had the dried-out feeling of one with a constant low temperature. The light from the stove showed flushed cheeks just like Mama's. Meenu had it, too! Meenu had Mama's sickness! Vashti wanted to cry.

Govind came through the doorway. "Something smells good," he said.

"It is fish and rice and we will all have guavas, too," Mama said.

"I brought candles," and Govind handed them to his mother.

"You are a good boy, Govind," she said, lighting one.

"Did you bring me a cigarette?" Mr. Prakash asked.

Scarcely giving him a glance, Govind tossed a cigarette toward his father. It landed on the floor and Mr. Prakash picked it up.

"You may light it for me," he said.

"I don't want Govind lighting your cigarettes. He will learn to smoke and he is too young for that," Mrs. Prakash told her husband.

To avoid another argument, Vashti held the candle so that her father could light his own cigarette.

When supper was ready, Mrs. Prakash filled a bowl with fish and rice and passed it to her husband. He accepted it and began eating as if he had not said he wouldn't eat food given by the Christian. The family waited until he had finished, as was the Hindu custom. Mama handed him a guava and then started to fill the other bowls.

"I'll have one of those oranges, too," Mr. Prakash said.

Mama passed him an orange and then served the others.

Govind had plunged his hand into his bowl. With his mouth full, he spoke to his sister. "Narayan thinks you are pretty."

While Vashti blushed, he turned to his mother. "Say, this stuff is good."

Later, when the bowls were washed and the mats were spread down for the night, Vashti and Mama and Meenu went outside.

"Who is Narayan?" Vashti asked.

"He is a child of darkness," her mother answered.

"You mean he is a bad one?"

"Yes. But good, too. He is the leader of a group of children who have no family to provide for them."

"And Narayan sees that they are fed? How does he do it?" Vashti asked.

"He lives by his wits, stealing, begging. He teaches them to do the same," Mama answered.

"It is a wicked way to live," Vashti exclaimed.

"But better than dying," Mama said quietly.

All the same, Vashti agreed with *Baba*. Govind

should stay away from Narayan. He had a family. He need not run with such a band of culprits. She wondered if her brother had become a thief, too. She was afraid he had.

Before Vashti went to sleep she remembered that this night was Christmas Eve for the Christians. Perhaps right now Radha was watching the play that told of the birth of God's Son. She went to sleep remembering the singing drama just as Radha had described it to her.

Mama got up early in the morning to get ready to go to her work. She and Meenu were eating a bit of rice held back from the night before when Mr. Prakash awoke.

"Well, Gauri, I see you lost no time putting on your fine clothes. I suppose you think you can draw the looks of men by flaunting yourself," he said.

"No, husband. I have no wish to be noticed by a man. And if I had, my good sense would tell me I am an old woman and no one would be attracted to me."

Vashti looked at her mother and her eyes filled with tears. Having been away, she saw her family with clearer eyes than she had seen them before. Mama was right. She was 29 years old, perhaps not as old as Miss Adhikari, but she was an old woman.

Meenu had slept with her doll and she held it now as she and her mother were about to leave the house.

"You look very pretty, Mama," Vashti whispered, standing at the door.

Her mother answered her with a smile and then she spoke to her husband. "You are not to send Vashti on the street to beg. It is not safe for one like her." She disappeared before Mr. Prakash had a chance to reply.

"Who makes the decisions in this house? I do!" he shouted after his wife. But not then nor at any time while Vashti was at home did he send her out to beg. Maybe he thought of all the money she would make when she finished school and thought the risk too great.

The days passed slowly for Vashti. She loved the time she spent with Mama and Meenu but she was cooped up most of the day alone with *Baba*. If he talked at all it was to carp upon the treatment he received at the hands of his family or to blame the gods for his fallen state.

Govind spent every day on the street. Each evening he gave a handful of *paise* to his mother. It was his begging money, he said. Some mornings he asked Vashti to go with him but she refused. Both Miss Narain and Mama had said she would not be safe. Besides, she had no wish to encounter the filth left on the streets.

Being in the house all day long gave her too much time to think and her thoughts always followed the same pattern. She worried about Mama's and Meenu's health. Mama coughed blood more often than she had when Vashti left for school. Someday she would die. Vashti would leave school and look after Meenu, but who would take care of her little sister until she could get here? Govind wouldn't know how. Besides, he would be out scrounging for *paise* to keep the family. *Baba* still referred to Meenu as the *bewakoof* and the child always sat in a dark corner as far from her father as possible. *Baba* had wanted Meenu dead when she was born. Without Mama, would Meenu be safe?

Vashti took over the cooking. The night before she

was to leave for school she cooked a special meal for her family. Hot red peppers, green peppers and dried lentils went into the pot along with the rice and she seasoned it well with spices. She used part of the precious wheat flour to make *loochi*. The fruit had been eaten since it wouldn't have kept any longer but there was chutney as one more treat for her last dinner at home.

When Mama came in she filled *Baba's* bowl and the rest of the family waited until he had finished eating.

Just as they were getting ready to eat, *Baba* said, "Vashti, your skirt will make a fine *dhoti* (garment) for your brother."

"But *Baba,* I can't give up my skirt. I have nothing else to wear," she exclaimed.

Govind rose to his feet and looked down at his father. "I'll not wear a *dhoti* made from a girl's skirt!" he shouted.

"You'll wear what I tell you to wear," Mr. Prakash shouted back.

Mama began to cough and Meenu clung to the folds of her mother's *sari*.

"*Baba,* you want me to go to school. How can I go if I don't have a skirt to wear?" Vashti asked.

"You will wear your old skirt, the one you wore before you went away. And your mother will make a *dhoti* of this one for your brother," her father said as though making a simple explanation.

"Her old skirt is gone. It was a rag and I threw it away," his wife said.

He jumped to his feet and slapped her across the mouth. "You lying wench! You covered the fruit with it two days ago. I saw it!"

140

Mama coughed harder and blood dribbled from the corner of her mouth. Meenu screamed and *Baba* struck her. She fell to the floor and crawled to her dark corner where she sat whimpering.

"Stop it!" Vashti shouted, unable to bear the fighting. "You have it your way, *Baba*. I'll wear the old skirt and Mama can make a *dhoti* for Govind from this one.

"No!" Govind shouted. "Keep your skirt. I'll not wear anything made from it. I'll never wear *dhotis* again. I'm going to wear Western pants." He dumped his food onto the floor and slammed out the door.

Mama knelt down and began scraping up what she could save of the rice and lentils. "We can't waste good food," she said.

As it turned out, no one but *Baba* ate Vashti's dinner that night and Govind was still somewhere outside when she finally went to sleep. Nor had he returned when she awoke in the morning.

"Where did Govind stay last night?" she asked her mother when they went out to the water tap together.

"Most likely, he was with Narayan. They have built a house of sorts from cardboard boxes and pieces of wood they found on the dump."

"Does he stay away often?"

"He is at home most nights," her mother answered.

Vashti felt discouraged and sad when she told her mother good-bye. It seemed to her that things were going very badly at home. Evidently, she wouldn't see Govind again before she left.

She tied the waistband of her old skirt together with a piece of string since the ends would not meet. "Good-bye, *Baba*," she said and went out of the house.

12

A Skirt for Vashti

When Vashti left home to start back to school she
found Govind waiting for her on the path that led to
the street. Across his arm he carried a pink skirt with a
gay band of red around the bottom.

"Put this on," he greeted her. "You can't meet Miss
Narain in that old rag."

"Where did you get it?" Vashti asked.

"What difference does it make? You had to have a
skirt and I got one for you."

"You stole it," she accused him.

"What if I did? It's just as good as if I paid for it with
rupees. Put it on," he said.

"I won't wear stolen things," Vashti told him.

"How else was I to get it? I'm only trying to help you." Govind daubed at his eyes, ashamed that he was near tears.

"Brother, I can't bear to think of you doing the things you do. You lived before you took to stealing. Must you do it now?" she asked.

"Stealing is a game. And it's exciting," he told her.

"Mama has a hard life without you adding to her worries," Vashti replied.

"Please take the skirt. I don't want the other girls at school to see you in that old rag," Govind begged her.

If her brother hated to have her look like a beggar, Vashti hated it too. But there were other things that weighed on her more heavily then her appearance. When she told Mama good-bye she wondered if she would ever see her again. Again, there was the fear of what would happen to Meenu.

"I will wear the new skirt if you will make me a promise," she said.

"What kind of promise?" her brother asked.

"Mama is very sick, Govind. It is her cough and she may die sometime. If this happens, I want you to promise me you will take Meenu to the Christian Brotherhood of Sharing. They will look after her."

Govind looked serious. "I didn't know Mama was that sick. I promise."

Vashti accepted the skirt. Stepping off the path, she slipped the new garment over her head, then broke the string of the old one and stepped out of it. Govind gave it a kick and they started walking toward Uncle Jogu's stall where they were to meet Miss Narain.

"How will I find the Christian Brotherhood of Sharing?" he asked.

"We'll ask Miss Narain how to get there," Vashti answered.

Vashti saw her uncle trying to attract a customer before she reached his place. She bore him no ill will. Surely he could not be expected to support the Kripal Prakash family just because *Baba* was his nephew.

"Vashti! Welcome to my shop. And you Govind, you do not come to see your old uncle. Have I treated you so badly?" he asked.

"No, Uncle. But I have no time to visit."

"And your father? I suppose he still considers himself too good for the work he is able to do?" Uncle Jogu asked.

"Baba sits," Govind answered briefly.

His great-uncle shook his head gloomily until he sighted a possible customer at the front of the stall. Then Uncle Jogu left his grandnephew and grandniece to use his persuasive powers for a sale. When the stranger walked on, Uncle Jogu returned.

"Vashti, you have become a pretty girl. Your *baba* should be looking for a husband for you," he said.

Uncle Jogu must be in his dotage if he did not realize there was no money to arrange for a husband for her, Vashti thought. Aloud, she said, "I don't want to marry, Uncle. I want to go to school and then work and use my education. Miss Narain is going to pick me up here and take me back to school this morning."

"Is that the lady of high caste who picked you up here before?" he asked.

Vashti nodded.

"My nephew's child is coming up in the world."

He left again when a tourist stopped to look at his glass bangles. He had no sooner returned when Miss

Narain came along. She stepped from her automobile.
"Good morning, *sri* (Hindu title equivalent to 'mister')
It is good to see you again," she said to Uncle Jogu.

He beamed and gave her an obsequious bow.

"Hello, Govind, Vashti," she said. "I'm sorry but we
must leave now. My motorcar is blocking traffic."

The din of a car horn proclaimed her right.

"Let me ride with you a ways, Miss Narain. We
must ask you something," Govind said.

"Climb in," she said. "But don't announce yourself
to your friend Narayan if you should see him. I don't
like him keeping pace on foot with the automobile."

She bowed to Uncle Jogu who stood before a customer and she, Govind and Vashti stepped into her car.

"Now, what did you want to ask me?" she said when
she had begun moving with the traffic again.

Govind looked at Vashti and the girl started to talk.
"Mama has the sickness that is called tuberculosis,"
Vashti said. "She works but she is very sick. If she
should die, there would be no one to look after my little
sister until I could reach home. I made Govind promise
to take her to the Christian Brotherhood of Sharing. Is
it all right?"

"It is all right," Miss Narain said.

"My sister is not bright like other children. She came
at a time of famine and Mama was too starved before
she was born to feed her brain properly. Is it still all
right?"

"It is more right now than ever that she should come
to the Christian Brotherhood of Sharing," Miss
Narain said.

"Can you tell Govind where the place is so he can
take her there?" Vashti asked.

Miss Narain fumbled with one hand to open her purse. She reached inside and drew out a card. "Can you read it?" she asked Govind as she handed it to him.

He was able to read everything printed on it.

"I see you haven't forgotten. You were a bright student in school, Govind. What is your aim in life, now? What do you want to do more than anything in the world?"

"I want to drive an automobile," he said.

"You'll never realize that ambition if you stay on the street. Think about it." She pulled as near to the curb as she was able. "You had better get out here. If you ride any farther, you'll be too far away to walk back."

"Good-bye, Miss Narain. Good-bye, Vashti."

"Good-bye, Govind. Write to me and tell me how all of you are. You can get my letters at Uncle Jogu's stall," Vashti said.

"Maybe I'll write if anything happens," he said.

He darted through the crowd, leaving Vashti to be satisfied with his half-promise.

Miss Narain didn't speak while she drove through the remaining *bustee*. When driving became less of a chore, she said, "Well, Vashti, I hope your days at home were pleasant. I see you have a new skirt."

Vashti colored but she made no reply.

"Want to tell me about it? You don't need to if you don't want to."

Vashti thought Miss Narain deserved some explanation since she had been the donor of the skirt *Baba* had appropriated.

"*Baba* made me leave the skirt I was wearing at home. He said Mama could make a *dhoti* from it for my brother. Govind was very angry. He left the house

147

last night and didn't come back."

"Where did he go?" Miss Narain asked.

"I guess he stayed with his friend Narayan. He met me this morning and he had this skirt. He said he didn't want the girls at school to see me wearing the old ragged garment I had on."

"That was kind of him," Miss Narain said.

"Yes." Vashti was quiet a moment, screwing up her courage to say what she must say. "I shouldn't have accepted it. He stole it."

"I presumed he had," her friend answered. "Almost all boys who must beg on the street come to stealing sooner or later. But when he took the skirt his motive was good."

"It was wrong of him to steal it. Do you think Govind is a wicked person?" Vashti asked.

"I can never approve of stealing, but I keep wondering which is more wicked, a boy who steals or poverty that drives him to steal."

"He is good to Mama. He gives her money to buy food. After she pays the rent there is not enough left from what she makes to keep the family from starving."

"I can't believe Govind is a bad boy. Maybe we can save him from himself," Miss Narain said.

"You mean you will try to find a job for him?" Vashti asked, filled with gratitude.

"Yes, it will have to be a job. We'll never get him back in school. I'll try to locate someone to hire him who will have a good influence over him," she said.

"You are so good!" Vashti exclaimed.

"No, Vashti. I only try to do what I can. But it is so little and India needs so much," she said sadly. Then she turned to the girl beside her and smiled. "The skirt is lovely. The girls will think so, too. You tell them your brother gave it to you. I don't see why you should tell them anymore."

13

Govind Gets a Job

Vashti said good-bye to Miss Narain at the school compound and then hurried to the hostel, eager to see her friends again. She heard a commotion of voices while she rushed up the stairs. When she came into the room everyone appeared to be talking at once.

"Oh, Vashti! What do you think? Shoba's engaged!" Radha greeted her.

Vashti looked at Shoba. "You're engaged?" she shrieked. For the first time since she left here she began to feel like a normal young girl again. "When did it happen?"

"While I was at home on holiday," Shoba said.

"She was just telling us about it," Purnima said,

while Vashti wondered how any of them had heard above the din.

"Go on. We want to hear the rest of it," Lata urged Shoba.

"No. Start all over again. I want to hear it from the first," Vashti said.

"All right, but I don't know why all of you are making such a thing of it. I've always known my parents would find a husband for me by the time I was 16," Shoba told them.

"But you aren't 16 yet," Vashti said.

"The wedding won't be for six months or maybe longer. But my father and my fiance's cousins compared our horoscopes and they harmonize," Shoba explained.

"How did you meet him?" Radha asked.

Shoba looked shocked. "I haven't met him. I won't until our wedding day."

Radha's excitement over the new situation visibly waned. Romance had escaped it like air from a pricked balloon. Having a minister for a father, she had lived too much within the Christian circle to have an understanding of the Hindu acceptance of arranged marriages. Some of the other girls who had always had friends of the Hindu faith as well as those of the Christian religion understood perfectly.

"How did your father locate him?" Lata asked. "Did he answer an advertisement?"

"No. My brother's wife's uncle works for the government putting in wells on farms and villages. My father asked him to keep his eyes open for a good match. He heard of a young farmer that seemed right so *Baba* asked him to act as a go-between."

"What is the name of your betrothed?" Vashti asked.

"Ram Nizam."

"Shoba Nizam." Vashti tried it out for sound. "It's pretty."

"Did you meet any of his family?" Shantha asked.

"His two cousins came to see me to pass judgment," she said.

"What were they like?" Radha asked.

"I couldn't look at them. It would have been unfitting," Shoba told her.

"Did you just stand in front of them with your eyes closed?" Radha pursued.

"Not closed. I looked at the floor," Shoba explained.

"Didn't you take even one little peek?"

"Of course not. I wasn't even curious. I'm not marrying the cousins," Shoba stated.

Radha looked as if the whole thing was beyond her. "I'm glad I don't have to have an arranged marriage. I want to know my husband and know that I love him before I marry," she said.

"I trust my father's judgment. He has my best interest at heart. And love will come after I marry," Shoba said.

"Will you have to live with his parents?" Purnima asked.

"We will live with his mother. His father is dead."

"Oh, then you will have to be submissive to a mother-in-law. I hope she is good-natured," Shantha said.

"I've always expected my husband's mother to teach me her way of cooking and keeping house," Shoba answered, her voice getting a little edgy.

"See here, I think all of you are asking Shoba too

many questions. She's engaged and I'm sure she'll be happy and I'm glad for her," Vashti exclaimed.

"You're right. I've asked too many questions and I wasn't very nice," Radha said. "I'm sorry, Shoba. I guess I never understood what it would be like to be a Hindu and follow the Hindu marriage customs."

"That's all right. I know ours are a lot different than the Christian customs," Shoba answered.

Later, Vashti and Radha paired off to eat their evening meal.

"Your skirt is beautiful," Radha said.

"Thank you. My brother gave it to me. Was your Christmas like you said it would be?" Vashti asked.

"Yes. It was wonderful. I thought I was so filled with love for Jesus that I could never hurt anyone again. Then first thing, I was not very nice to Shoba."

"She'll be all right. Do Christians really fall in love before marriage?" Vashti asked.

"We don't go out on dates like Western couples do in the movies. But we have boyfriends who call on us and we have a chance to make up our minds whether or not we will marry the one who calls. We aren't likely to marry against our parents' wishes, though."

"Do you have men calling on you when you are home?" Vashti asked.

Radha laughed. "No. I don't intend to marry until I am 20. And I won't marry then if I don't find someone I want."

Marriage, as Radha had spoken of it, offered a whole new concept to Vashti. It caused her to think more seriously about Hindu marriages, too. What if two people married, never having seen one another, and one of them objected terribly to the appearance of the other? What if Ram Nizam couldn't bear the sight of the pockmarks on Shoba's face?

Next day, she and Mrs. Ghose were working side by side in the garden, clearing away some old vines and dead plants.

"Were you and Mr. Ghose Christians when you were married?" she asked the older lady.

"No, little one. It was later that my husband and his family and I listened to the missionary. Then all of us became Christians."

"If you weren't Christian, did you have an arranged marriage?" Vashti asked.

"Yes, a real old-fashioned Hindu marriage. Our fathers matched our horoscopes and agreed upon the dowry. Then *Baba* consulted the astrologer to make sure of the right day for the auspicious occasion."

"Didn't you see one another before the wedding?" she asked.

"No. To do so was unthinkable," Mrs. Ghose answered.

"When your husband saw you did he—I mean what did he think—"

"I think you are trying to ask me if my dark skin made a difference," the older woman said kindly.

"I guess I am," Vashti answered.

"It may have been a surprise, but it was not an unsurmountable obstacle. My father offered a fine dowry and that pleased his family. For my husband's part, well, from the very first I made him comfortable. I rubbed his feet and scratched his toes. When his mother permitted me to cook, I fixed the dishes he liked best. And every day I gave him a clean white

155

dhoti to wear. He is a good man and we have a good marriage."

"I can see that," Vashti answered. "I just wondered how it was at first."

"You are thinking about Shoba's marriage. Those two will accept one another and adjust to their new way of life. A dark skin, a pock-marked skin, what is the difference when the wife works to please her husband?" Mrs. Ghose asked.

"None, I guess," Vashti answered.

"Shoba may never know the romantic love some girls dream about, but very likely there will be a growing together that will bind them tighter than their wedding vows," Mrs. Ghose predicted.

Shoba was so matter-of-fact about her coming marriage that the other girls couldn't keep up their sense of excitement for long. Never a giddy sort of girl, she did her work and applied herself to her studies just as she had always done.

Vashti considered her a good friend. She was the only girl of the Hindu faith Vashti knew here at school and it created a bond between them. On Sunday afternoon, they still walked to the temple of Mitra in Lorabad where they offered a little of their noontime rice and made their supplications.

These trips left Vashti strangely unaffected. She had no feeling of satisfaction upon leaving the temple. It was as if she gave lip-service only, although she tried hard to reach the god, Mitra. Sometimes she felt she would have been better off staying at the school compound and going to afternoon chapel meeting there. Although she wasn't a Christian, Miss Adhikari's talks, the stories she told about the Master, were an inspiration to Vashti. Many times when things didn't go right or she was discouraged she would find herself thinking of Jesus. Would He be discouraged? How would He expect a Christian to act if that person faced her problems?

Her problems were the worries she carried from home. Govind was one of her major worries. It wasn't only that stealing was wrong. He might be arrested by the police. But her mother's cough was her real concern. She couldn't bear the thought of Mama dying, but if it should happen and Govind took Meenu to the Christian Brotherhood as he had promised, Vashti knew she could not leave her there. She would go home and take over Mama's duties, which meant going to work as a sweeper as well as caring for Meenu and *Baba* and Govind. Work as a sweeper! What a dreary future! How heartbreaking it would be to leave school before she had finished.

Such thoughts always sent her flying to her books. She must learn everything possible while she had the opportunity. Radha was in seventh grade now and Vashti borrowed her books and read them whenever she had a little time.

"Before you know it, you will be in my class," Radha said one day.

"I'm the same age you are so I ought to be in your class," Vashti answered.

"You'll probably be in eighth grade before I get there," Radha told her.

"No, I won't. You're smarter than I am. Besides, you said English is used in all the eighth grade classes and that will stop me. I don't understand it when it is spoken," Vashti answered.

"Then we'll have to practice it. Let's start using nothing but English when we eat together," Radha said.

"That would be fine with me but I'm afraid you'll get tired of being my tutor."

"Of course I won't. Besides, I'll be getting some good practice myself," Radha said.

From then on, they spoke only English at mealtime except for the words Vashti had to use in Hindi because she did not know the English words to use in their place. Radha would supply it and Vashti would repeat it. The Christian girl was very patient correcting Vashti's pronunciation and sentence structure and always speaking slowly so that she could be understood.

Sometimes Vashti went home with Mrs. Ghose and stayed overnight. As they walked to school next morning, Vashti almost always had some question to ask her older friend about the Bible passage she had listened to the night before.

"Little one, have you ever thought of becoming a Christian?" Mrs. Ghose asked her once.

The question took Vashti by surprise. "Oh, no," she answered hurriedly. "*Baba* would never allow it."

One afternoon, Miss Adhikari sent word for her to come to her office. A very pleasant surprise awaited Vashti there. It was Miss Narain.

"Hello, Vashti. I had business not far from here and I thought I'd come by and see how you are."

"I'm fine, Miss Narain," she answered. Her welcoming smile proved it was so.

The principal spoke. "Miss Narain would like to take you into town. She knows of a nice restaurant there but she doesn't like to eat alone," Miss Adhikari said.

Vashti's big eyes grew bigger. "Eat in a restaurant?" This would be a new experience for her. But then she realized she couldn't go. "But Miss Adhikari, I have to stay here and milk."

"I'm sure someone can handle your milking this one time. Run along and enjoy yourself."

"Thank you," Vashti said, beaming.

Miss Narain took her hand and they raced as if they were both schoolgirls to her automobile.

After entering Lorabad, Miss Narain said, "Let's sit in the park a while. I have something to tell you."

Vashti searched her friend's face and her smile widened. "I'm sure it's something nice or you wouldn't look so happy."

Miss Narain returned the smile but she said no more until they were seated on the grass under an asoka tree.

"Your brother Govind is working," she announced.

"Oh, Miss Narain, I'm so glad. What is he doing?" Vashti asked.

"He is working at a garage washing cars. That's what he was hired to do and what he is doing. But on his own, he is making himself generally useful. He follows the head mechanic around and hands him the tools he needs and does anything else he sees that he can do," Miss Narain told her.

"Does he get paid?" Vashti asked.

"Yes. At least as much as he brought in from begging. And he will learn to fix automobiles so that one day he can work as a mechanic."

"He'll like that. I'm so grateful to you. He doesn't have to live where he works, does he?"

"No. The owner gives him his bus fare extra and pays him every day so he can give your mother money when he gets home at night."

"He must be a good man. The owner, I mean," Vashti said.

"He is a good man. A good Christian," Miss Narain said.

"Does *Baba* know the garage is owned by a Christian?"

"I don't know. Govind is pretty independent and probably wouldn't quit the job no matter what anyone said. He is staying away from Narayan and that pleases your father."

"It pleases me, too," Vashti answered.

They left the park and Miss Narain took her young friend to the finest dining place in Lorabad. Vashti was overawed by the sparkling cut glass in the chandeliers, the painted decor of the walls, the lovely *saris* of the ladies sitting at the table next to them. But not too overawed to enjoy being there. She watched Miss Narain and mixed her sauces with the food as she saw her do. Everything looked exotic and tasted even better.

When the last crumb was gone, Miss Narain said, "Now I must get you back to the hostel. You must have studying to do for tomorrow."

Going back, Vashti knew she would always remember this evening, but the best part was the news about Govind.

14

Fire in the Night

A dog chasing a cat ran between Mrs. Ghose's legs and threw her down. When she picked herself up, a pain shot through her foot and she found she couldn't stand on it.

"I'm going for the doctor," Hari Ghose said. "Your ankle may be broken."

"I think there is no need to get the doctor, husband. I'll be all right by morning," Mrs. Ghose said.

Her mother-in-law examined the foot. "A hot mustard plaster is all Mutu needs," she told her son. "The heat will draw out the swelling."

"I'm going for the doctor. Your ankle may be broken," Hari Ghose repeated and climbed on his bicycle and rode away.

The doctor declared the injury a sprain and bound the ankle and foot tightly. "Stay off it for a week," he said as he left.

"My buffaloes! Who will take care of them?" Mrs. Ghose exclaimed in dismay.

"Miss Adhikari will find someone," her husband said soothingly. "You lie here like the doctor said and don't worry about anything at school."

He went to the principal and explained his wife's injury.

"I'll get someone from town to take over her work," Miss Adhikari assured Mr. Ghose.

"She wanted me to tell you that she always gives the *arnas* a good rubdown after the milking."

Miss Adhikari gave a half-smile. "I know. She tends them so well that she spoils them. Assure her that there will be someone to feed them and rub them down. Vashti will do what she can to hold down the weeds in the garden until your wife gets back."

Miss Adhikari asked her friends in Lorabad if they knew of a reliable person who would look after her four buffaloes for a few days. She would rather have a woman than a man but she couldn't locate one who had worked with buffaloes. It was late in the afternoon when a rather rakish young man presented himself at her office door.

"You are looking for someone to care for your *arnas*," he said.

"Yes. Have you worked with them before?" she asked.

"I have. We had *arnas* when I was a boy and milking was my chore," he told her.

162

She had misgivings about him. He slumped indolently while he toyed with a packet of cigarettes he held as though wanting to get away so that he might light one.

"There is more to the work than milking," she said. "If that were all, the girls could handle it. There is the feeding and I shall want you to rub down each buffalo before you leave," she said.

"I'll do it," he agreed.

"Very well." She wasn't happy about hiring him but it was too late in the day to try to find anyone else. "I'll go with you now and show you about."

He lit a cigarette as soon as they left the office. She looked at him sharply.

"Put that out before we reach the milk shed. There will be no smoking on the job. With so much hay around, it is dangerous."

The man drew in a few deep breaths of smoke, exhaled and dropped the cigarette in the path. He crunched it under his foot to extinguish the fire.

Miss Adhikari showed him where the fork was kept and pointed to the stack of hay near the milk shed. "Feed them now and I'll show you how much to give them," she said.

Before he was through forking the hay, the principal saw the three girls, Vashti, Lata, and Shoba, coming to milk. Each girl carried a vessel on her head and Vashti carried a second one—Mrs. Ghose's—in her hand. With a strange man there, Miss Adhikari thought it would be best to stay with the girls until they finished their milking. Every evening after that she came with them and stayed until they were through.

One evening, as they approached the milk shed, she

saw the man she had hired carrying a forkful of straw while a lighted cigarette dangled from his lips.

She hurried ahead. "You were told there would be no smoking on the job," she said. Her eyes flashed.

He dropped the cigarette and stamped it well into the ground.

"There, you see it is out and no harm done," he said.

"Don't light another," she warned him. "Not at any time you're working here."

Later that evening, while the girls were in their room studying, Vashti lifted her head and sniffed.

"I smell smoke," she said.

"So do I," Radha agreed.

Lata called from her end of the room, "Vashti, you don't suppose that man . . ."

Shoba was halfway downstairs and Lata followed her.

"What is it?" Radha asked.

"The man who feeds the *arnas,*" Vashti explained as she headed for the stairs. "He was smoking this evening."

All of the girls in the room rushed to the courtyard. The night was dark and clouds overhung the sky for a storm had been brewing all day. When they looked toward the milk shed they could see nothing.

"The smoke must be coming from Lorabad," Shoba said. "If we had a fire here we could see the blaze."

They trooped back upstairs and began studying again.

The acrid odor became more pungent.

"That smell is too strong to be coming from Lorabad," Vashti said. She started downstairs and again all the girls converged in the courtyard.

164

Suddenly the moon broke through the clouds and they a saw a billow of smoke down the path near the milk shed.

Vashti, Lata and Shoba broke into a run but Miss Adhikari passed them as they raced down the path.

Sparks were shooting up now and soon a sharp tongue of flame brightened the sky. They could see that it was the haystack afire, the haystack that stood so near the shed housing the *arnas*.

"The buffaloes!" Miss Adhikari gasped, speaking to the three girls who were milkers. "Those flames will reach the barn and we must save them."

The girls from the hostel had followed them and the light from the fire showed teachers here and there pushing through the group toward Miss Adhikari.

"Miss Dal," the principal said to the mats teacher. "Will you go to my apartment and telephone the fire department?"

Miss Dal left at a run.

"And you other teachers, will you find every vessel anywhere about the school and have the girls fill them with water? But don't let anyone go too near the fire."

Now Vashti heard the *arnas* stomping inside their shed. Their blatant bawling carried the sound of terror-ridden beasts. She could imagine her buffalo throwing its head wildly. She flinched at the thought of going near its long-pronged head. In her imagination, the animal that had held no fear for her three hours earlier suddenly became a dangerous brute.

If the firemen would only get here and put out the fire! Maybe they were on their way now. The burning haystack could surely be seen even in Lorabad.

She was aware that Miss Adhikari and Shoba and

Lata hadn't yet made a move to enter the milk shed either. It must be especially terrifying to Miss Adhikari because she wasn't accustomed to being around the *arnas*.

Now there was a sharp crackle of flames and a burst of sparks seemed to explode into the air. They drifted downward between the hay and the shed. The fire illuminated the area around them and they could see as well as if it were daylight. Dry grass where the sparks had landed sent up a beacon of smoke. Miss Adhikari rushed to the spot and stomped the ground, stopping what would have been the start of another fire.

Judging from the noise inside, the smoke and loud-popping flames had driven the *arnas* nearly crazy.

There was fear in Miss Adhikari's eyes but her voice was firm. "We can't waste any more time. We must go in there and untie those animals and lead them out. The poor beasts will burn if we don't."

Thinking how terrible death by burning could be, Vashti moved forward. When she reached the shed door Shoba was close behind her. The four entered. Fire glow from outside cast an eerie light over the interior. Glints of red and white played intermittently on the *arnas,* some pawing the earthen floor and snorting, others lifting their heads and bawling.

"You take that arna, Miss Adhikari," Vashti said, indicating her own. "I'll take Mrs. Ghose's." Then she moved like a sleepwalker to the animal that was making the greatest fuss.

She remembered how Mrs. Ghose had told her to begin making friends with the buffaloes by stroking them. She was afraid to come close enough to this fear-struck animal to stroke it. She went to the front where it was tied by a rope. Seeing her, the buffalo stepped back, rolling its eyes wildly and pulling the knot tighter. She began speaking to it softly, using the same soothing words Mrs. Ghose used when she petted it. She thought it appeared a little calmer. She began working at the knot but her fingers couldn't budge it as long as the rope was drawn taut. She leaned forward and tugged at it gently. The creature took a step toward her and then stopped. Her fingers found the knot and began loosening it. The light flared brighter through the door. The animal threw its head and Vashti lost what she had gained in untying the knot. Somehow, her nearness to the buffalo allayed her fears. She reached forward and began to soothe it, stroking its face. It became more calm.

"There, little one. You're my pretty one and we're going to get you out of here." She might have been Mrs. Ghose herself, murmuring to the frightened beast.

At last she was able to untie the rope. She led the *arna* without trouble until she tried to take it through the door. Half out, the smoke, the crackling flames, the light now bright, now red, sent new fear through the animal. It recoiled and would go no farther.

Vashti saw Lata behind her, waiting to take her own buffalo through the door. She simply must get this beast out of the shed and into the open. Still holding the rope, she put her arms around its neck and began talking into its ear. All of a sudden, Lata's buffalo threw back its head and let out a terrific bawling noise. Vashti's nervous animal leaped forward while she still embraced its neck. She clung to it a little ways, then tried to race ahead of it but she couldn't even keep up

with it. She tugged and the animal pulled, heading straight for the garden. Sometimes she found herself being dragged on the ground, then she would get to her feet only to be pulled down once more. But she held onto the rope and the buffalo finally quieted and came to a stop. Vashti felt its quivering sides. She rubbed it silently while she looked for the others. They were all here in different parts of the garden. She and Mrs. Ghose would find it a mess but the *arnas* were safe.

"Oh, Vashti! You would be the one to lead out Mrs. Ghose's *arna* when you know it's never been as gentle as the others," Lata scolded her.

"It wasn't too hard to get out and someone had to lead it," Vashti answered.

"Not too hard! And you were dragged at the end of the rope halfway here," Lata exclaimed. "You must be scratches all over."

Vashti was too busy holding onto her restive animal to examine herself for scratches.

Miss Adhikari and Shoba were standing together a distance away.

"We'll tie up the buffaloes in the courtyard," the principal called to the other two girls. She waited for them to join her.

"How do you think the fire started, Miss Adhikari? That man put out his cigarette. Do you think he came back and did it deliberately?" Lata asked.

"No. I think a spark fell into the stack when he was forking hay and it smoldered a long while before it really caught."

When she could take her attention from her buffalo she turned to look at the fire. She saw the girls like shadows dousing water into the flames.

The principal looked frantic. "I didn't want them trying to put out the fire themselves. Some of them may get burned. I must hurry!"

"Go to them. We can tie up your *arna*," Shoba said. She reached for the lead rope and Miss Adhikari ran down the garden path.

Before she reached the girls the fire leaped to the milk shed roof. The wood was old and very dry. The flames appeared to chase themselves across its length dropping burning embers into the hay inside.

"Leave, girls. You can't do any good now. Come away!" Miss Adhikari shouted to them. To her relief, they left the burning shed and came to meet her.

"You should never have gotten so near the fire," she scolded them. "Some of you could have been hurt."

Now the storm clouds that had hung darkly all day opened up and the first raindrops fell. Soon, rain came down in torrents and Miss Adhikari knew the fire would not spread any farther. There was little need for the fire department when it arrived.

The principal called all the girls and teachers to her. "We will bow our heads and thank God that all of us, and the *arnas* too, are safe," she said.

After the prayer, they dispersed to their rooms and went to bed.

It was time for the April vacation, April and May, actually, since everyone would be away 45 days.

Miss Adhikari sent for Vashti.

"Would you like to work in Lorabad during the holidays?" she asked.

Vashti was quick to answer that she would.

"A young couple would like to have a girl to look after their two small children. The lady isn't well. It will be an interesting experience for you and they will pay you a small salary."

"When do I start?" Vashti asked. She hadn't forgotten that she had promised *Baba* she would bring him a present next time she came home. Now she could manage it and maybe get herself a new blouse and skirt.

"You'll start as soon as classes end. And Vashti, Radha told me you had been reading her seventh grade books. There will be time for you to study while you are staying with this family. I'll give you books to take along. If you can pass the seventh grade tests before school resumes, you may start the new term in eighth grade."

"Thank you, Miss Adhikari. Thank you very much."

School, she thought, was wonderful. Everyone connected with school was wonderful. There was only one small shadow to sadden her. She was losing her friend, Shoba. The wedding date had been set and Shoba was leaving school for good.

15

Thou Shalt
Have No Other Gods

The address on the envelope was a childish scrawl.
Until she saw it, Vashti had forgotten how much
further she had gone in school than her brother,
Govind. She sat down on the floor beside her cot to
read her letter.

Dear Vashti, I said I would write if anything
happened.
Well, Meenu is dead.

Meenu dead? Vashti had never considered that her
little sister might go before Mama.
"No, no, no," she murmured, clasping her arms

about her knees and rocking back and forth. The tears rolled down her cheeks and fell on the pink skirt Govind had given her. Poor little Meenu! Starved before birth, she had never had enough food to become really strong. But how had she died? She returned to Govind's letter.

She was sick two days and then her spirit left her body.

I am working at a garage. Miss Narain found the job for me. Some day I will fix motorcars but now I wash them.

The owner of the garage took Meenu to the furnace for the dead in his automobile so she wouldn't have to go on the city truck. Mama and *Baba* and me went along. I rode in front.

Good-bye, Govind

When she finished reading Govind's letter she still did not know the cause of Meenu's death. Probably Govind knew no more than he had written. Meenu was sick; she died. The family would not have called a doctor. Doctors cost money and they had none. For an instant Vashti wanted to beat someone with her fists. What kind of a world was it that would let her little sister die because her family had no money, not even a few coins, to pay for medical care?

Her anger soon receded. Did Meenu find life so good that she would wish to stay here and endure it longer? In her rebirth she would surely be far better off. Now she remembered the belief of the Christians. If one followed the Master, one would go to be with Him when life was ended here. Meenu had always been a good child. Might it be possible that the Supreme

174

God would take her to the Christians' Heaven?

Vashti ached with the wish that she might have seen her one more time. The house would seem empty without little sister when she went home again.

She got up and sat on the edge of her cot and reread Govind's letter. Her brother's Christian employer was a kind man to take little Meenu to the crematorium in his car. The thought that her sister's body might have been tossed up on the city truck with other dead bodies set Vashti trembling. She lay down and spilled her tears of grief into the coverlet of her cot.

Radha came upstairs and found her there. "What is it?" she asked, full of concern.

"Meenu is dead," Vashti sobbed.

"Your little sister? Oh, I am sorry," Radha said.

Vashti sat up and wiped her eyes on her skirt hem. "Do you think she could possibly be in the Christian Heaven?" she asked.

Radha almost jumped in her surprise. "I-I'm sure I couldn't say. I'm not smart enough to know the answer."

"But could it be possible?" Vashti asked.

"I suppose it could be. What made you think of it?"

"Jesus seems like such a comforting person and Meenu will miss Mama so much. And Mrs. Ghose's Bible tells us He said, 'Suffer the little children to come unto me and forbid them not . . . ' "

" 'For of such is the kingdom of Heaven,' " Radha finished for her. "I can't say she is with Jesus but I can't say that she isn't."

Vashti seemed satisfied since Radha hadn't made a flat denial. She went downstairs to the tap and washed her face. Then she came back to her room and picked up her books. She was in eighth grade now and she had no wish to fall behind the rest of her class. But the words on the pages blurred so that she couldn't study on this day.

Except for Shoba who was married now, all of Vashti's friends were back in school after the long holiday. The girl who took Shoba's place in the hostel room was a Christian. This left Vashti the only one professing the Hindu faith among all the girls there.

When she had first come to school it had meant a great deal to her to know that Shoba was a Hindu. Now she gave no thought to the fact that all her close friends were of another religion.

Without Shoba to walk with, she had almost given up her visits to the temple of Mitra. It seemed so natural to go with the group to Sunday afternoon chapel. She had never stopped to ask herself where all this was leading. She knew only that the hymns, the Bible reading and Miss Adhikari's talks fulfilled a need within her.

Valli Kutar was a new little girl in school. She was assigned to a room where most of the girls were her own age. She came because her father was sent as a representative of his company to London and her mother had, of course, accompanied him.

But the couple had wanted their daughter to be educated in their native land of India. It wasn't right that she should grow up knowing only the strange ways of a foreign country.

Although they were of the Hindu faith, they had chosen Miss Adhikari's school because they had heard the boarding students were well cared for.

This was important since Valli was only seven years old.

Vashti watched the child and wished sometimes that she might have occupied Shoba's bed. There was something about her that reminded the older girl of her little sister, Meenu. She wasn't quite sure what it was, maybe it was only her size and the fact that she came to school about the time Vashti learned that little Meenu was gone. But she thought it was more than that. There was a wistfulness about Valli that made Vashti want to protect her.

One Sunday Valli missed the noontime meal. Miss Adhikari kept a close check on the younger boarders and she asked others who lived in her hostel room if she was ill. They said she was not in the room. They had thought she was outside.

At first, Miss Adhikari assumed she was somewhere inside the school compound. She called the older girls and asked them to make a thorough search. They fanned out, some going through all the classrooms, some searching outside the buildings, some going over the grounds. The little girl was still missing.

"We must conclude that she has gone outside," Miss Adhikari said. "I shall have to phone the police in Lorabad and ask for their help."

She sent word to the different hostel rooms that there would be no Sunday afternoon chapel until after Valli was found. She went, herself, to the room where the little girl lived.

"Did Valli say anything that would give us a clue where she might have gone?" she asked.

"No," one of the girls answered. "She didn't talk very much."

"Did she seem unhappy?" Miss Adhikari pursued.

"Maybe," one girl said.

Now the little girl who slept in the cot next to Valli's spoke up. "She cried at night. I guess she missed her mother."

"She wouldn't try to go to her mama. She knows her mama is not at home," another child said.

"Thank you, girls. And don't worry about her. I'm sure she can't be far away," the principal told them.

She went out and spoke to one of the teachers. "I think the child might be on the road leading to Ranchi. That is where she came from. I'm going to drive slowly along the road and look for her. If the police come, give them any information they need."

"Can't some of us girls go into Lorabad and hunt for her?" a student asked.

"I'd rather you didn't. I described her to the officer at the police station and I'm sure he'll send his men out to look for her."

Miss Adhikari went for her automobile and drove away.

Vashti pictured the little girl, alone and homesick, trudging along the road. Her heart ached for her. At least this was something Meenu had never known. All of her short life Mama was with her to love her and keep her safe. Valli's parents must have plenty of money but this was no consolation for the little girl who cried at night.

A policeman came to inquire what the child was wearing. The girls in her hostel room hadn't seen her leave so they couldn't tell the man.

Miss Adhikari returned. She had seen no sign of the missing girl. She called to the child who had the cot next to Valli and they went upstairs together.

Miss Adhikari took down all the skirts and blouses the child had brought with her.

"Look at them carefully," she told the small girl. "Think hard and tell me what clothes are missing."

The child looked them over and finally said, "She had a white skirt with pink dots in it and a plain pink blouse. They aren't here."

"You've been a big help," Miss Adhikari told her. She went downstairs to phone the description of the clothes to the police on duty at the station.

While she still sat there at her desk, Vashti came to the outer office. "Come in, Vashti. "Can you suggest any place where we might look for Valli Kutar?" she asked.

"That's why I came," Vashti told her. "When I first came here, I was homesick and all of you seemed so strange to me because you are Christian and I am of the Hindu faith. I thought if I could just pray to our family goddess, I would feel closer to those at home. Even though Valli is so little, she might be looking for a place to worship. She might even be at one of the shrines right now."

"It's something to go on, anyway. I'll telephone the police again and suggest they go to all the shrines in Lorabad. When you and Shoba went out on Sunday afternoon, where did you go?"

"To Mitra's temple," Vashti said.

"You and I will drive there as soon as I have talked to the man on duty at the station," Miss Adhikari said.

She told Miss Dal where they were going and she and Vashti left.

They pulled up at the curb and hurried to the temple.

They saw her before they reached it, a little bundle of pink and white, kneeling at the feet of Mitra. Her head rested on the stone above. She was sound asleep.

Miss Adhikari gently awakened her. "Valli," she said. "We thought you would be tired after your long walk here. We've come to drive you back to school."

The little girl stood up and reached for Miss Adhikari's hand. "I had a hard time finding the temple. I asked people where it was and they told me, but I always got lost. I had to walk and walk."

In the car, she leaned against Vashti and slept all the way back to the school compound. They roused her when they arrived.

Miss Adhikari rang the bell that called the girls to chapel.

"Our little girl is found. We will have a short service now and thank God that she is safely back," she said.

After the meeting she told Vashti she would like to talk to her. Vashti followed her to her office.

"I am troubled that a child must run away in order to worship in the way she has always done. Tell me honestly, did you miss your religion terribly when you first came here?" Miss Adhikari asked.

"I remember that I did. I wanted to pray for my mother. She works as a sweeper but she is ill. I didn't know where to go and I was afraid to ask. I thought a Christian school might not permit us to worship our own way even if you did permit us to go here to school."

"I see," Miss Adhikari said. As though thinking aloud she added, "We take a child from its family and put her where she no longer has access to her form of worship. This could make her feel that she has nothing firm to hold onto."

"I soon met Shoba and went with her to Mitra's temple," Vashti told her.

"I think perhaps we should appoint a big sister for every girl coming in as a boarder. And a Hindu girl must have a big sister who is Hindu," Miss Adhikari said.

Vashti felt she should act as a big sister to Valli whether or not she was appointed. She had felt like crying when she saw that tired little girl asleep at the feet of Mitra. But if she took Valli to the shrine every Sunday afternoon she would have to miss chapel. Still, she was of the Hindu religion and not Christian and it was only right that she should worship and take Valli to worship at a Hindu temple.

"I will take her to the shrine after this, Miss Adhikari. She is much too small to go alone," she said.

"You have been coming to Sunday afternoon chapel, Vashti," the principal said.

"But I am Hindu. I should go to the temple."

"Very well, if that is what you want to do."

Vashti hadn't thought she would mind going to the temple of Mitra the following Sunday afternoon but she found she did. It was almost as if a power beyond her strength to resist was drawing her to the chapel. But Valli met her in the courtyard and reached trustingly for her hand. She couldn't fail the child. They started walking toward Lorabad.

Both of the girls had held back some of their midday rice. When they reached the temple, Valli went forward and made her offering, then bowed low to make her supplication.

FAITH REFORMED LIBRARY
ROUTE 3 — BOX 19
KANKAKEE, ILLINOIS 60901

Vashti approached the stone god slowly. When she came to the base she held out her offering but a feeling of repugnance swept through her and her body went stiff. She tried to kneel but she couldn't bend her knees. "Thou shalt have no other gods before me!" This surely was not spoken within her own head. It seemed to reverberate all around her. This was the command of the Christian God but she was Hindu. What did it all mean?

Suddenly, she was filled with happiness. It meant that she, too, was a Christian! She believed in God, the Father, and in His Son, Jesus Christ! With this revelation, all rigidity went out of her body. She wanted to shout to the skies that she *believed*. She turned and ran from the temple, her arms outstretched as though wanting to embrace the whole world, so great was her joy in her new knowledge. The pigeons behind her feasted on the rice she had brought as an offering to Mitra.

She was in a hurry to get back to school and tell of this wonderful thing that had happened to her. She waited impatiently at the curb until Valli joined her. Taking the little girl's hand, she started walking. It was almost impossible for her to slow her pace to that of the younger child.

When she had left Valli at the hostel she went straight to Miss Adhikari's apartment.

"Come in, Vashti," the principal said when she answered the knock. She thought the girl looked strangely radiant. "You look different. Are you all right?"

"I am different and I am all right. I will always be all right now because I am a Christian."

"Oh Vashti, I am so happy. Need I tell you that is what I have always wanted? But when? Tell me about it," Miss Adhikari said.

"I knew when I went to the temple of Mitra. You see, I couldn't bow down to the image and suddenly I knew why. I believe in the One God and in His Son, our Master," Vashti explained. Each word was touched with reverence.

"How wonderful!" Yet Miss Adhikari knew that sooner or later Vashti would have to face some serious opposition, but she wanted her to hold to her buoyant mood as long as possible. "Go now and tell the girls in your room. You will want to share this great moment with them. Then come to my office in the morning before you go to class. We have a lot to talk about."

Vashti hurried away to tell of her newfound joy to Radha and her other friends.

16

No Longer a Daughter

Next morning when Vashti came again to Miss Adhikari she looked much more serious than she had the evening before.

"You have had time to reflect on the changes that will follow now that you have turned to Christ, haven't you?" the principal said.

"Yes," Vashti agreed. "I must tell *Baba*. I can't go home and pretend that I am still of the Hindu religion when actually I am a Christian. But you know he has forbidden me to become a follower of Christ."

"Jesus did not promise that the Christian's life would be an easy life," Miss Adhikari told her. "But you have courage and the Master's help."

"*Baba* will put me out and I will never see Mama again," Vashti said sadly.

"If it happens it will be hard for you but you will come back here. It isn't as if you will be homeless," the principal consoled her.

Vashti's eyes filled with tears. "All my life I have depended upon my mother. When I was little, no matter how bad things were, she took care of me. And Govind and *Baba* and Meenu, too. I lost my little sister when she died. Now I will lose Mama."

"But there is a happier side," Miss Adhikari pointed out. "You have found Christ. No matter where you are you will never really be alone again because you have Him."

The thought brought comfort to Vashti. "Do you know Radha knew I was a Christian before I knew it myself? When I told her she said she was glad it had been revealed to me because she had known it for a long while."

"Radha is a good friend," the older woman said.

"But how could she know it when I hadn't known it?" Vashti asked.

"She lives with you and she watched the transformation within you. You didn't know it because you could not admit the change even to yourself since your father forbade it."

"Do you think I will be able to go home at Christmastime?" Vashti asked.

"I think so. You will tell him then?" the principal asked.

"Yes, I will tell him. No matter what happens, I will tell him."

Last year, Vashti had heard the story of the birth of

the Baby Jesus. This year, her belief in the Child gave Christmas a greater meaning. She wished she might have lived at that time and have seen Him. However, she knew this was not necessary. When she came to believe, she was like a new person wanting to serve Him.

And yet Christmas had its measure of sadness. She felt sure her trip to Calcutta would bring about the final break with her family. Never to see them, never to know if Mama was sick or even living, seemed at times more than she could bear.

Her hostel room again became a beehive of activity in preparation of Christmas gifts for the families of the girls. Vashti was making a *dhoti* and *kamis* (shirt) for her father. She had spent most of her last summer's earnings for the material so he would not feel neglected. She still had a little money and she would buy some *jelebies*, too. They would be a treat for the whole family. Poor Mama must be content with a blouse Vashti had made from one of her old skirts. Perhaps Govind could keep back enough of his pay to buy her a *sari*. Mama needed a new one badly.

While she sewed Vashti remembered Meenu's delight in the doll she had taken to her last year. She had to stop her work sometimes to wipe the tears from her cheeks. How she wished she could see her little sister on this trip, perhaps her last trip, home. But her new Christian religion gave her comfort here. No longer believing in reincarnation, she felt sure Meenu was with Jesus. A just God could never hold it against a poor backward girl like Meenu that she had not accepted Christ. Little sister had never heard of Christ and couldn't have understood if she had been told.

Vashti had many talks now with Miss Adhikari. She looked to her for guidance in the Christian religion.

"When will I be taken into the church?" she asked.

"We won't plan your baptism or church membership until you return from Calcutta. There is always the hope that your father will approve the change within you. In that case, Miss Narain will arrange the baptismal ceremony at the Christian Brotherhood of Sharing so that your parents can be present. If this doesn't work out, we will have the ceremony in the chapel here at school," Miss Adhikari said.

"Will you baptize me?" Vashti said.

"No, I cannot. I am a teacher, not a minister. I've talked to Mrs. Ghose and she said her pastor will come to us and perform the rites. You will be taken into the church after your baptism."

On the morning of December 23, the principal asked Vashti to come to her office.

"Miss Narain will be here soon to drive you to Calcutta. I don't want you to feel cut off from all of us so I am giving you bus fare to Lorabad if things go badly for you at home."

"You are very good to me," the girl said.

Miss Adhikari put her arms around Vashti. "You'll be in my prayers," she said.

"I will remember. Thank you."

In the car when Miss Narain and Vashti were on their way to Calcutta, Miss Narain said, "I had real reason to rejoice when I heard you had become a Christian. It's what I've always hoped for."

"I'm glad, too," Vashti answered.

"But you fear what will happen when you get home, don't you?"

"Yes. I'm afraid *Baba* won't let me stay," Vashti said.

"I will be at my parents' home for Christmas but I want to give you the telephone number of the Christian Brotherhood of Sharing. If your father makes you leave, you can phone them and they will come for you."

"I won't need to phone them," Vashti told her. "Miss Adhikari gave me money for bus fare back to school if I can't stay at home until you come for me."

"Perhaps that would be better. You wouldn't want to be with strangers at such a time," her older friend admitted.

They reached Calcutta while the bazaar was still open for business. Again Miss Narain shopped with Vashti, filling two big bags with the best of spices, fruit and other delicacies.

"Please, Miss Narain, don't spend all that money on us," Vashti said.

"I want to. I want to do all that I can to soften your *baba's* attitude toward Christians," Miss Narain answered.

"I don't think it will help. Last time he said he wouldn't eat food that had been touched by Christian hands," Vashti told her.

"And did he eat it?"

Vashti gave a wan smile. "Yes." She grinned more broadly. "I was afraid none of the rest of us would get a taste of the fruit."

"So you see my point. He says things he doesn't really mean. And even if his daughter turns to Christianity he may not be as harsh as you fear."

"I hope you are right," Vashti answered.

Once more Vashti found herself in the hated *bustee*. Miss Narain let her out of the motorcar and she picked

189

her way through the debris and the sad souls abandoned there by fate. She turned down the path near the brick store and followed it until she came to the hut that housed the Prakashes.

"Hello, *Baba*," she said. Entering from the daylight outside, she could scarcely see in the darkness.

"Well, Vashti. So you take time to see your *Baba* again, do you?" he asked in greeting.

"Yes, *Baba*. It is our December vacation and I have come."

"What is it that you carry?" he inquired.

"It is the gift of fruit and other things from Miss Narain," she said. She also carried the presents she had made for him but she wanted to wait until Mama came before she opened that package.

"You can peel me an orange," he said.

"Yes, *Baba*." She peeled the orange and handed it to him.

He bit into it and the juice ran down his chin. "It is not as sweet as the oranges you brought last year."

"I'm sorry, *Baba*. Miss Narain bought the best they had at the market."

Finishing off the fruit, he licked his fingers. "You said you would bring me a present when you came again," he reminded her.

"Yes, but I want to wait until Mama comes before I open my package. I'll go to the tap for water now. It will help Mama if I have the fire going and the water hot." She took the water vessel and went outside.

When she came back she found *Baba* sitting with his new *kamis* and *dhoti* spread out on the floor. He was chewing *jelebies* while he squatted, busily counting money.

190

It was her emergency money Miss Adhikari had given her! How would she get back to school now?

"You are a good daughter. You brought all these *rupees* for your *baba*. Now, Govind need not toss a cigarette at me as if I am a beggar."

She dared not ask him to return the money. To do so would hurry along the crisis. But what was she going to do?

"Yes, *Baba*," she answered meekly. She told herself it was her own fault. She should have hidden the cash in the clothing she wore and not tied it up in the package. All she could do now was hope for the best.

She stirred the coals and added fuel. Mama would soon be home.

At sight of Mama when she came in, Vashti burst into tears. She thought she was prepared to face the loss of her little sister, but seeing her mother without Meenu at her side brought it all back too vividly.

"Vashti!" Mrs. Prakash exclaimed. She went to her daughter and held her close.

Although her mother was always the soul of kindness, Vashti could not remember when she had last made a gesture of affection toward her. It was as if a tacit agreement of love existed between them and they had no need to display it. Looking at her now, she saw rivulets of tears coursing down her face through well-worn creases. Vashti lifted her hand and wiped the wetness from Mama's cheeks.

"I wish I could have seen her again," she said.

"I miss her all the time," Mrs. Prakash answered simply.

She moved now to the end of the room where she did her cooking.

"Miss Narain sent more fruit and spices and a fish," Vashti told her.

"That was kind of her. I'll fix the fish for supper," her mother answered.

Mr. Prakash demanded attention now. "Look what Vashti brought me, clothes and *jelebies* and money. Now I can buy all the cigarettes I want and betel nut, too," he said.

His wife looked inquiringly at Vashti, but she answered, "Yes, husband."

"Yes, husband," Mr. Prakash mimicked her. "Is that all you have to say when our daughter has shown what a good girl she is? I suppose you are too anxious to fatten yourself on the food the Christian woman sent," he said.

"I will fix the fish with rice and chili and a few spices and you will like it, too," she said.

"Like the fish when it came from the Christian? It will stick in my throat," he answered.

Mrs. Prakash made no reply but set about preparing the evening meal.

When supper was almost ready, Govind came home. He came in sniffing. "Fish and spices. Vashti is home!" he exclaimed.

"Hello, brother," she greeted him.

"Hello. I didn't know you were coming."

"I didn't write. I don't think you go to Uncle Jogu's to get my letters. You never answer them," she said.

"I wrote to you once," he reminded her.

"I know. I thank you for letting me know about our little sister," she told him.

"I don't have any time to write. I am working hard and learning to be a mechanic," he said.

192

"It is true," Mrs. Prakash said to her daughter. "You see how late it is when he comes home. But sometimes it is much later."

"The man at the garage takes advantage of him," his father said.

"He is a good man," Mama told her husband. "He is helping Govind to learn so that he can make more money."

As Mrs. Prakash talked she filled her husband's bowl and handed it to him. Vashti saw there had been changes made since she was home last year because now Mama filled Govind's bowl, too. Only mother and daughter waited while the two male members of the family ate. Well, this was as it should be. Govind was 12 years old and bringing home regular wages. Vashti began peeling fruit for the two of them.

When supper was eaten, Mama collected the bowls and cooking pan and she and Vashti went outside to the water tap to wash them.

"Mama, I must tell you something because I want you to know before I tell *Baba*. I am now a Christian," Vashti said.

Her mother grabbed her arm. "No, Vashti! Don't say it. He will put you out and I can't bear to lose both my daughters."

"This is the part that makes me feel bad, Mama. But I must say it. I don't believe as a Hindu now. I can't pray to the Hindu gods. And that is because Christ is in my heart. If I don't turn to Him, I don't have anything."

Her mother didn't answer but she was overcome with a coughing spell.

"I'm sorry it has to be this way, Mama. Maybe *Baba*

won't disown me. He knows I will make quite a lot of money when I get through school."

"It won't make any difference," her mother gasped. "Govind and I make enough money now for him to live as he wants to live." Mama stopped and gave herself up to coughing again. At last she was able to go on. "Don't tell him now. Put it off until you are ready to leave. Let us have this time together."

"All right," Vashti agreed. She thought it could do no harm to put off the telling. As they started back, she said, "I didn't give you the present I made for you. It is a *choli* I cut from a skirt of mine. I'll give it to you when we go in."

As night closed down upon the Prakashes in their one room, Vashti tried many different positions before she found one that would bring sleep. It was not because the mat on the floor was hard after being accustomed to sleeping on a cot at school. It was because she hadn't told *Baba*. By now she should have made her stand for Jesus. But surely He would understand that she owed a few days to her mother. Mama asked so little from life but she had asked for time with Vashti.

The next morning when she had seen her mother out the door her heart beat faster. Govind had already left for the bus that would take him to the place where he worked. Vashti must spend the whole day alone with *Baba*. She must watch what she said lest she arouse him to anger. She wanted to stay away from the subjects of school and religion.

By busying herself, washing *Baba's* old garments and cleaning the house, she was able to get through the day. Rice was ready when Mama came in.

When Govind hadn't come at the usual time, *Baba* said, "The boy is going to be late again. I'll have my supper now."

Mrs. Prakash filled his bowl and handed it to him.

"I'll fix your fruit for you, *Baba*. What kind do you want?" Vashti asked.

"What kind did the Christian buy for us?" he asked.

"There are oranges, guavas, bananas, mangoes and pomelos," Vashti said.

"The fool spends plenty of *rupees* trying to bring you over to her foreign religion," *Baba* said.

Vashti made no answer.

"I'll have a pomelo and an orange and a banana."

Vashti began to fix the fruit.

"It won't do her any good, will it, Vashti? You wouldn't take up with unbelievers, would you?" he asked.

Vashti tried to avoid a direct answer. "I think Miss Narain gave us the fruit because she is a nice person. I don't think she had any other reason." She handed her father a banana.

He took a large mouthful and then began talking before he had swallowed it. "You didn't answer me, daughter. I have forbidden you to become a Christian and you mind me, don't you?"

"I mind you in almost everything," she murmured.

Baba leaped to his feet and stood over her. "You are a Hindu!" he shouted. "You remember that. You cannot turn Christian!"

She was quiet for a moment except for her knees that were quaking. This was the time, she knew. Now she must tell him.

"You cannot turn Christian. Do you hear?" *Baba* repeated. "I forbid it!"

195

Vashti closed her eyes and prayed that the Master would give her strength. White-faced, she turned then and confronted her angry parent. "You are wrong. I can because I have."

Now that she had said it, she felt strong enough to face an army. She saw her father raise his hand and she didn't flinch.

The blow came down so hard across her face that she fell to the floor. He stood over her, livid with anger. "You are not a Christian. You are a Hindu. Say it," he ordered her.

She answered from where she lay. "I can't say it, *Baba.*"

He kicked her viciously. Then he limped back to his mat and sat rubbing his bare toes.

"Gauri, we have a strange girl in our house," he said, turning to his wife. "Put her out."

"No, husband, she is our daughter. The only one we have. She brought you money and clothes. Let her stay," Mrs. Prakash begged.

"I can't be bought as she was bought. Put her out."

Defying her husband, Mrs. Prakash stood resolutely beside Vashti who was on her feet again. "I won't," she answered him.

He was up from his mat in an instant and struck his wife hard across the side of her head. Vashti caught her as she fell. She eased her gently to the floor. Mrs. Prakash began to cough. Her daughter held her head upward till the worst had passed.

She turned to her father. "I am going now, *Baba.* I forgive you for disowning me because I know you think you are right. Maybe someday I will be a good enough Christian that I can forgive you for hitting

196

Mama. Now I'm not that good. I feel like I hate you for that."

Her father started to rise again. "Why you . . ."

Vashti glared at him. To his own surprise he found himself sitting down again, not finishing what he meant to say.

After she had put her few belongings together she walked toward the door. She took a last look at her mother who was struggling to hold back her tears.

"Good-bye, Mama. I'll always love you. Tell Govind good-bye for me, too."

Mrs. Prakash tried to answer but her coughing stopped her.

17

Alone in the Dark

When Vashti stood in darkness outside the hut that had once been her home, she thought of the *bustee* streets and how she hated to walk there even in daylight. Must she now join the homeless derelicts and spend the night sleeping there?

She was half-inclined to wait where she was until Govind came home. But why should she wait for her brother when she had Christ now? "Master, speak to me. Tell me what I must do," she prayed.

Uncle Jogu. Yes, she would go to Uncle Jogu who had given the whole family shelter when they had first arrived in Calcutta. Even though *Baba* had only mean things to say about the older man, Vashti had never blamed him because he had asked the family to leave. After all, he was old. Why should he support them? And Uncle had always been kind to her in his own grumpy way. She started walking through the night blackness toward the main path that would lead to the street.

She hoped she could avoid the human waste some child or adult may have left on the ground but it was too dark to see where she stepped. Her only guide was the darker shapes of the other houses and an occasional glimmer of a candle inside.

She reached the path and turned to walk straight ahead knowing she would come out at the street. Hurrying, wanting to get to the safety of Uncle Jogu's stall as quickly as possible, she walked straight into an object and fell. She was not frightened. The warmth, the animal grunt, told her one of India's many unclaimed cows had bedded there. She walked around the beast and continued on her way.

As she neared the street she passed a family grouped together and, farther on, several men who were gathered around a small fire for warmth. As she went by, one of them left the group and walked behind her.

At first, Vashti thought nothing about the one who followed. Then she noticed that if she walked faster he walked faster. If she slowed her pace he slowed his. He was so close!

What did he want? Why was he after her? When Miss Narain urged her last year not to go out on the street alone was it because of men such as this one? Govind had said his friend, Narayan, thought she was pretty. Was this man attracted to her, too? Was that why he followed? She was sure that his reason was not the same as the young men Radha told her about who came to call on Christian girls. She hurried faster, breaking into a run, then fell over a sleeping man who lay under his coverlet in the middle of the street. Like the cow that had blocked her path, the man grunted but paid no further attention to her. She was on her feet and running again but she heard her pursuer running behind her.

People were all about her, the homeless who lived on the street, clustered together now, cooking, eating, talking, sleeping. They paid no attention to a young girl who was fleeing from a man. And yet their nearness gave her a certain amount of safety. He could have grabbed her any time but he hadn't. He must be waiting until he had no witnesses. Vashti hoped she could make it to Uncle Jogu's stall before anything happened.

And then he grabbed her. His arms encircled her from behind and his hands moved over her thin blouse. She felt as if this awful person had made her dirty. In her panic she resorted to the instincts of an animal. She sunk her teeth into his groping hand and bit down until she knew the warm salt taste of blood. He let out a cry of pain and loosened his hold upon her. Instantly she was running again. She kept running, never noticing the man had ceased to follow her.

When she reached her uncle's, she was panting for breath. His stall was shut down for the night.

"Uncle Jogu," she called. She knew he was awake. She saw the light of his lantern showing through the bamboo slats that closed him in.

His slow footsteps approached. "Is it Vashti?"

"Yes."

He unlatched the gate and she entered the circle of light where he had been counting his day's earnings.

"You shouldn't be out so late by yourself," he scolded her.

"I had to come, Uncle Jogu. I had nowhere else to go," she said.

"You're trembling. What are you afraid of? Did my lazy nephew beat you?" he asked.

"A little but it isn't that. A man followed me. And he grabbed me." She started to cry.

"What could you expect, a girl like you on the street so late at night? Why do you come here?" he asked in his carping way.

"*Baba* turned me out," she said, hoping he would not demand the reason why.

"Oh, he did, did he? And like all the Prakashes, you neglect your uncle until you need him and then you come."

"I'm sorry, Uncle. But I just got here yesterday," Vashti told him.

His tone became gentler. "Well, it makes no difference when you came. A young girl like you can't stay by herself on the street. Take down a mat and find a place to sleep for the night," he said.

"Thank you, Uncle Jogu," she answered.

Early next morning, while she stirred the coals to a blaze to cook the day's rice for the old man, Govind arrived.

Uncle Jogu let him in.

"I couldn't find you last night," he said, addressing Vashti. "And then I thought you must be here and I went home. What are you going to do now?"

"I want to go back to school. But *Baba* took the

money the principal gave me for bus fare. I'll have to start walking," she said.

"You can't walk there. It's too far." He turned to Uncle Jogu. "Can't you loan her the money?" he asked.

The old man looked shocked. "Loan her money? How could she pay me? These people, they let her go to school but they don't give her as much as a *paisa* to do so."

"I will pay you," Govind told him.

"Big talk. And how will you do that? You are paid a beggar's salary for your work," his uncle said.

"I will pay you when I get to be a mechanic. I will make more money then than you make here in your shop," Govind told him.

"And in the meantime?" Uncle Jogu asked.

"I'll pay you interest. I'll hold back some of the money from Mama."

The thought of a loan with interest frightened Vashti. It was the loan her grandfather had taken that had brought about the downfall of the family.

"No, Govind. There is no need for money. I am strong and I can walk," she said.

Uncle Jogu dropped his caviling tone. "I will give you money and neither of you shall pay me. I am not as miserly as you think. I do this because you two prove the Prakashes haven't become a nothing," he told them.

Now, Vashti felt she couldn't take the money from Uncle Jogu without telling him why she found herself in the predicament she was in.

"I must tell you this . . ."

"No!" Govind interrupted her.

"Yes, brother, I must." Turning to the old man,

she said, "Uncle Jogu, I don't believe as a Hindu any longer. I am a Christian."

"And it is for this your *baba* put you out," he said, understandingly. "Well, I have lived a long while and in those years I have known Christians. I saw much good among them."

"Then you will still give her money?" Govind asked.

In answer, his uncle began counting out *rupees* and putting them in Vashti's cupped hands.

Govind watched, counting each one as it was transferred. When his uncle stopped, Govind said, "That isn't enough. A bus ticket will cost more than that."

Uncle Jogu favored him with a crafty look. "It will take her near enough. A few miles' walk is small enough price for a Christian to pay."

Govind thought about it and then he grinned at his uncle. "You are right," he agreed. Looking at Vashti, he said, "Come on, sister. I'll take you to your bus but we must hurry or I'll be late to work."

"Good-bye, Uncle Jogu. I'll always remember how kind you were," she said.

"Oh, here," Govind said, thrusting a bag into his uncle's hand. "I brought you some 'Christian fruit.'"

When they were out on the street, Vashti said, "What will *Baba* think when he asks for an orange?"

"He'll think someone stole his 'Christian orange,'" Govind answered with a wide, disarming smile.

When they reached the bus, Govind said, "Well, good-bye. I must catch my own bus, now."

"Govind!" she called to his retreating back. "You will write to me, won't you?" Her voice held a pleading note.

"I'll write but not often. I'm not a scholar," he said.

"It is Christmas Day," she thought as she found a seat on the bus. She remembered the story of Christ's birth and all He had come to mean to so many people, even an unworthy person like herself. But this thought reminded her of the events of the last few hours and tears spilled down her cheeks. The bus had filled and they were moving now. She didn't want the occupants to see her crying. She concentrated on Govind and she smiled remembering how the "Christian fruit" had found its way to Uncle Jogu's. How she would miss her lively brother! In spite of him seeming older than his years in some respects, he had a boyish spirit and an enthusiasm for living that the *bustee* would never dampen. Perhaps Govind's Christian employer would influence him so that he, too, would become a Christian. She would write to her brother and urge him to let her have news of Mama. He was the link between herself and home.

Still thinking of Govind, she fell asleep because she had slept little the last two nights. She was awakened by the bus driver.

"This is where you get off, Miss," he said.

She took the small package that held her belongings and stepped out onto the street.

She knew where she was and which way to go from here to reach the school. She had passed through this town with Miss Narain every time she had come from home. She was about ten miles from Lorabad and she would make it easily before the sun went down.

She started down the road walking rapidly. She looked out across the countryside and tried to think about the small villages and farms she saw there. Her mind wouldn't cooperate. The nearer she came to the school compound the more she felt the loss of her mother. Would she ever see Mama again? She couldn't hold back the tears thinking about her. Mama was so good, so gentle, and she had always looked after the family no matter what the conditions.

She broke her rapid stride and stepped off the road to pray. "Dear Jesus, help me now. Help me to realize my sacrifice is nothing compared to Yours. Please fill me with so much love for You and all mankind that I will not miss my family. Amen."

She didn't know whether it was a good prayer or not but her heart seemed eased a little.

It was then that she saw the child. She was a little girl sprawled on the ground under a eucalyptus tree. She lay so still that Vashti couldn't tell whether there was any life in her. She wore only a pair of panties and the bones in her rib cage stood out so plainly you could count each one.

Vashti went to her and she could see that the child still breathed. But she was plainly starving and someone had left her to die where she lay.

She stirred a little when Vashti picked her up in her arms. The older girl carried her as carefully as she could, knowing how easily her poor flesh could be bruised.

Vashti had two miles to go and though the child was little more than skin and bones, she felt very heavy before Vashti had walked a quarter of the distance. She sat down and rested. The trouble was, the girl was too tall for Vashti to carry easily. When she started out again, she tried carrying the load on her back, but this didn't work because the unconscious child couldn't

hold on, and Vashti was afraid she would let her fall. She laid her down again and when she picked her up she carried her in a sitting position, leaning the little one's head across her shoulder. It was awkward but it made the going easier. By resting a few times, she came in sight of the school.

Because she had been slowed down, it was later than she expected it to be when she turned in at the gate. Even though it was Christmas Day, Mrs. Ghose had come to the school because the buffaloes had to be milked. She was just leaving for home.

"In dear Jesus' name, what have you there, Vashti?" she asked.

"It is a little girl. Someone left her to die," she answered.

"Poor child. Poor dear little child," the older woman said, lifting her gently from Vashti and turning back toward the school.

Together they went to Miss Adhikari's apartment.

"Vashti dear, I see you have come back. But what have you here, Mrs. Ghose?" she asked.

"A starveling Vashti found along the way. I thought we would try to give her a little water," Mrs. Ghose said, laying the child down on a settee.

"Look at her bones! Her poor pitiful bones! Oh, God, spare her," Miss Adhikari exclaimed.

Mrs. Ghose went to the tap and brought back a gourd dipper filled with fresh water.

"Now, if you will hold her up so she won't choke," she said to the principal.

Miss Adhikari did as she was asked and Mrs. Ghose squeezed the little girl's cheeks, pushing her mouth into a round O. Drop by drop, she let the water fall into the opening. The child made the effort of swallowing.

"I would like to take her home with me. We will have the doctor come and see if she can be saved. And Mama Ghose will be happy to have a patient to care for," Mrs. Ghose said.

"You mean your husband's mother. She has been a practical nurse, hasn't she?" Miss Adhikari asked.

Mrs. Ghose nodded.

"I think we should let Mrs. Ghose take her, don't you, Vashti? Undoubtedly, she will have better care than we can give her here."

"Yes. I know Mama Ghose will take good care of her," Vashti agreed.

She watched while her older friend picked up the starved child and, holding her tenderly, went out the gate of the school compound.

Miss Adhikari brought her back to her own situation. "You haven't eaten, have you, Vashti? I had a nice Christmas dinner and there is plenty left here for you."

When she had placed Vashti at the table with a good meal in front of her, she said, "I'm sure you have a lot to talk about but you look very tired tonight. Nothing is so important but what it can wait until morning. Enjoy your supper and then we'll say good night."

18

A New Family

Next morning, Vashti came down the hostel steps and watched for Miss Adhikari. When she saw her leave her apartment, she followed her to her office and knocked on the door.

"Come in," the principal called out.

Vashti appeared tired-eyed and droopy.

"You look as though you didn't sleep much last night. Were you worrying about the little girl you brought here?" Miss Adhikari asked kindly.

"Yes. And I did a lot of thinking, too." Vashti paused and then blurted out, "Miss Adhikari, I'm going to quit school."

The principal's eyes widened but she showed no

other sign of her surprise. "May I ask how you came to that decision?" she said.

"I'm going to keep the little girl myself. I'll work to support her. She will be my family," Vashti answered.

"Let's go back a little way, Vashti. I take it that you told your father you were giving up the Hindu religion; he turned you out of your home. If he hadn't, you wouldn't have come back so early."

Vashti nodded.

"You still intend to hold to your belief in one God and His Son, Jesus Christ. Is that right?" she asked.

Again the girl nodded.

Did you pray about your decision to quit school?" the principal asked.

"No." The girl's answer was almost inaudible. She didn't tell how she had tried to have a conversation with the Master so she could explain why she must leave school. It had been like talking to herself. She hadn't gotten through to Jesus at all.

"There is so much you have to learn, Vashti. A Christian doesn't make any important decisions without seeking guidance from the Master," Miss Adhikari told her.

"But I prayed to Him yesterday. I prayed that He would always keep me mindful that the sacrifice I made giving up my family was not as great as the sacrifice He made for us," Vashti answered.

"That was a very fine prayer," Miss Adhikari said.

"Well, right after that I found the little girl who had been left to die. Last night it seemed to me I was meant to find her and keep her as my own."

"Do you feel Jesus spoke to you and told you this?" Miss Adhikari asked.

212

Vashti looked down at her feet. "No."

"How would you support her?"

"I'm 14. I could work as a sweeper," the girl answered.

"And bring up the child in a slum. Is that the kind of life you want for her?" Miss Adhikari pursued.

"Well, I would have her to love and she would be alive. She wouldn't have been if I hadn't found her and carried her here," Vashti said.

"You don't know that. Perhaps someone much more able to care for her than you are would have found her and given her a home."

Vashti couldn't say this wasn't true. She could say, "But I did find her."

"Vashti, you are putting too much importance upon having a family of your own. Don't you know that all of us are children of God and this makes all of us one family? True, some of us are poor and some of us are rich. Some of us have no skills and some of us have great talents. You were chosen by God to be especially blest. You have a very fine brain. Do you intend to waste it?"

Vashti made no answer and Miss Adhikari continued speaking. "It isn't as if you are the only one to care for the child. We don't even know if she will survive, but you surely realize that Mrs. Ghose and myself will provide for her if she does."

"I guess I was wrong to think she was mine," Vashti admitted brokenly. "She will have a better life if you two look after her."

"Don't feel badly, Vashti. You will have a better life, too, when you are educated and go out to do the work God planned for you to do," Miss Adhikari said. "Now

go and get yourself a bowl of rice and when you've eaten come back here. I want to tell you of my plans for you after you finish high school and go on to college."

"College?" Vashti asked.

"Yes, college. You were meant for big things, Vashti, and you have two friends, Miss Narain and me, who intend to see that you achieve them."

The smile Vashti gave Miss Adhikari gave light to both their faces.

"You and Miss Narain have always been good to me. Now I think I can face anything if I know I can go to college," she said. She left to go to the kitchen for her breakfast.

When she came back to the office, she found Mrs. Ghose there.

"Good news for you, little one. The doctor said our starveling has every chance to get well. Her heart is strong. It will take nursing and loving care but Mama Ghose is there to give her both. Already she opens her eyes and looks about."

"I'm glad. Has she had any food?" Vashti asked.

"Thick rice water last night and chicken broth this morning," Mrs. Ghose told her.

Chicken broth! Vashti understood then how poor her care would have been. She would never have had money to buy a chicken for her.

"She is lucky to be with you now," the girl told the older woman.

"We talked about her last night, husband, Mama Ghose and I. We want to keep her as our own." She looked from Miss Adhikari to Vashti. "If you are willing," she added.

The principal looked to Vashti and saw the last bit of

215

wistfulness fade from her eyes. "I am willing. I know she will have a good home," the girl answered.

Miss Adhikari nodded agreement.

"Then it is settled. And now to other important things. All of us are happy because you have accepted Jesus, little one. The day you are baptized and received into the church will be a day for us all to rejoice."

"Maybe Christ was in my heart for a long while but I didn't realize it until I found I couldn't bow down to a Hindu god," Vashti answered.

"But we feel sadness, too, that you have lost your family. You have been a joy to us when you have visited us in our home. I wonder if you could think of us as your relatives now?" Mrs. Ghose asked. Her voice was gentle as though she were pleading for herself.

Vashti hesitated only a second. "I could think of you as my aunt," she said.

"That would please me very much. And you would have an Uncle Hari and a Grandmama Ghose," the older woman said.

Miss Adhikari smiled happily, knowing Vashti would have help in crossing the bridge of loneliness. She took the girl's hand. "What fine new relatives you have," she said.

Vashti smiled, too, shyly at first and then broadly. "I think so, too," she agreed. "And I wonder if I might go home with Aunt Mutu tonight so I can see my little Ghose cousin?"

"How about it, Mrs. Ghose?" Miss Adhikari asked.

"There will always be a bed at our house for our little Vashti," she answered.

"Thank you, Aunt," Vashti answered. God's gift of life was a wonderful gift even though it held its portion of sadness. And soon Radha and all her other schoolmates would be back. Aside from the blessings of the present, there was a whole future of usefulness to look forward to. It was good to have Christ, it was good to have friends, it was good to be alive.

GLOSSARY

Angocha: scarf.

Arna: species of Indian domesticated buffalo.

Atman: essence, or spirit.

Baba: father.

Baksheesh: begging word, gratuity, tip.

Bangles: bracelets.

Bewakoof: idiot.

Brahman: Hindu of the highest caste—priests and scholars.

Bustee: slums.

Caste: hereditary social classes of India; there are five main classes ranging from Brahmans to Untouchables.

Choli: short-sleeved blouse worn with sari.

Chula: stove.

Churail: evil spirit.

Dhoti: skirtlike garment worn by Hindu men; often put on pulled up between the legs.

Ghee: butter.

Guntha: land measure (like an acre).

Hindi: official language of India.

Hindu: follower of Hinduism.

Hinduism: religious and social system prevalent in India.

Jutka: bicycle cab.

Jelebies: Indian candy or sweet.

Kamis: men's shirt.

Kali: goddess of evil.

Kshatriya: second highest Hindu caste—rulers and warriors.

Lakshmi: goddess who rose from foam of the sea.

Loochi: fried wheatcakes.

Mitra: Indian god of light whose name means "friend."

Namaste: an Indian greeting meaning "peace"— hands are raised to the chest and clasped together.

Outcaste: one who has been ejected from his caste.

Paisa: bronze coin worth 1/100 of a rupee.

Palla: end of sari, part worn over the shoulder.

Panchayat: group of elders who settle village affairs.

Pilau: rice boiled with fish, fowl or meat.

Ramayana: Indian epic that tells the story of Prince Rama and his attempts to rescue Sita, his wife, who has been kidnapped by the demon king Ravana.

Rupee: silver coin or paper currency of India.

Sardar: nobleman.

Sari: draped length of fabric worn as a dress by Indian women.

Ser: an Indian unit of weight (like a pound).

Sri: Hindu title equivalent to "mister."

Sudra: the fourth caste—unskilled workers.

Sweeper: a maid in a home or cleaning woman in an office.

Tata: grandfather.

Tiki: round dot worn on forehead by Hindu women of high caste.

Untouchable: person so low he has no caste, a non-Hindu—to touch such a person was a defilement to members of higher caste.

Vaisya: third caste—agricultural and merchant class.

FAITH REFORMED LIBRARY
ROUTE 3 — BOX 19
KANKAKEE, ILLINOIS 60901

The set of b is a much-appreciated gift.

Those who know the Bible will love the pictures; those who see the pictures will love the Bible!

Vol. 6—THE CHURCH: Acts to Rev., with a special section tracing the history of the modern Bible.

You can order these books from your local bookstore, or from the David C. Cook Publishing Co., Elgin, IL 60120 (in Canada: Weston, Ont. M9L 1T4).

---------------Use This Coupon---------------

Name ——————————————————————————

Address —————————————————————————

City ——————State ——————ZIP Code ————

ITEM	STOCK NO.	PRICE	QTY.	ITEM TOTAL
Vol. 1—CREATION	73080	$1.25		$
Vol. 2—PROMISED LAND	73098	$1.25		
Vol. 3—KINGS AND PROPHETS	73106	$1.25		
Vol. 4—THE CAPTIVITY	73114	$1.25		
Vol. 5—JESUS	73122	$1.25		
Vol. 6—THE CHURCH	73130	$1.25		
SET OF ALL SIX	73262	$6.95		

POSTAGE & HANDLING CHARGE
Please add 25¢ for the first dollar, plus 7¢ for each additional dollar, or fraction of a dollar. Minimum charge: 40¢. Maximum charge: $7.50.

Sub-total $ ——————

Handling ——————

TOTAL $ ——————

THE
PICTURE BIBLE
FOR ALL AGES

Do you have ALL SIX books?

Vol. 1—CREATION: Gen. 1 to Ex. 19. All the action from "In the beginning" to the Flight . . . in pictures!

Vol. 2—PROMISED LAND: Ex. 20 to I Sam. 16. Moses, Ten Commandments, wanderings, fall of Jericho.

Vol. 3—KINGS AND PROPHETS: I Sam. 16 to I Kings 21. Shows David and Goliath, wisdom of Solomon.

Vol. 4—THE CAPTIVITY: I Kings 21 to Mal. Covers the Babylonian captivity, prophecies of Jesus' coming.

Vol. 5—JESUS: Mt. to John. Dramatically shows the birth, teaching, miracles, final triumph of Christ.

(Cont.)